Nine stories of relationships on the edge, with dilemmas to face, secrets to be revealed and decisions to be made.

Decisions which will change the lives of each of the main characters forever ... but will they have the courage to decide, as they sit at the table in the taverna by the sea?

These stories are set in the beautiful, romantic Ionian islands of Greece. Sunshine, warm seas, blue skies and wonderful, welcoming people.

© Phil Johnson 2015

Phil Johnson asserts the moral right to be identified as the author of this work.

All rights reserved. No part of this publication may be reproduced, stored in retrieval systems, copied in any form, or by any means, electronic, mechanical, photocopying, recording or otherwise transmitted without the permission of the author.

This is a work of fiction. Names, characters, businesses, places, events and incidents are either the products of the author's imagination or used in a fictitious manner. Any resemblance to actual persons, living or dead, or actual events is purely coincidental.

Thanks:

To Fi, for everything.

Also to Sarah Louise Dean, Andy Murrow, Annabel Huxley, Nick Crane, Karen Reynolds, Paul Nettleton, Mark Smulian and Christy Lawrance for advice and encouragement.

Credits:

Editor - Lynn Curtis.
Proof reader - Emma Adams.
Book production - Paul Drummond.
Cover Photo - Fiona Johnson.

Dedicated to the memory of
Michael Belmore.

Contents

The Standby Wife – 1
Can a pact made in the past offer a hope for the future?

Broken Bikini – 13
A search for love, a mother's secret and a rock star's revelation.

Falling Stars – 30
Actors from a top TV Sit Com meet 10 years after a night they'll never forget.

Family Secrets – 45
A daughter's last goodbye reveals her parents' smouldering secrets.

Making Baby – 54
The search for a surrogate, a perfect donor, but a desperate decision.

Back to the Start – 67
Should you risk everything to go back and find a love you lost?

Westminster Wife – 78
He cheated. She's crushed. Now, it's time to fight back!

Cast Off Couple – 93
Three relationships, two couples, and one big decision!

Backstage Backstab – 105
Lust, loss and love inside one of the world's biggest rock bands.

The Standby Wife

The waiter at the taverna by the sea watched a middle-aged man stare anxiously at his watch. His second cappuccino of the morning stood before him. He was sitting at the table by the water, the one at the front with a view over the bay, waiting for the small ferry to come into harbour and tie up at the quay.

She'll be here when the ferry arrives... It's been so long since we really touched... I hope this isn't a wasted journey... Both of us have travelled out here to the island, to meet on neutral ground, just to see if this could really happen. She's on her way.

It's a long way to come but then we are looking at spending the rest of our lives together. Or are we? Maybe it'll just be a "friends with benefits" trip? Or even just a "friends" trip. Maybe we'll both realise it's a mistake, like you can on a first date. Well, it's a date all right, but with someone I used to know, someone I used to love and want, someone I think I want and need again now.

This coffee is really good. The island is as lovely as I'd hoped it would be; warm, inviting, surrounded by this bright blue sea. Very romantic. Well, that's why I suggested it, I guess. If it can't happen here it then can't happen anywhere... but maybe that's a mistake. Maybe we should meet somewhere cold, damp and depressing, let a little reality in. It won't always be like this: sunny, warm, fun. God knows, though, we've both been in the depths of loss and depression. Why not just grab at this, grab at having something, someone, anyone? Someone to believe in, someone to love.

I wonder what Danielle's thinking now. She'll know what I'm thinking. After all, she read psychology, and works as a clinical psychologist, so no hiding my feelings from her then! She'll probably be able to read me like a book. See straight through me. She always could. She seemed so mysterious to me once, so strong and such a resilient person. Her photo showed that she'd changed. Thinner, greyer, older, I guess. Mind you, mine was hardly flattering. Why do we betray our bodies so badly? More to the point, why do they betray us, let us down and reveal our fragilities and weaknesses?

Just another hour now and she'll be here. Unless, of course, she's changed her mind and pulled out. No, please, don't even think that! Just don't. I keep hearing my own pulse; keep feeling my heart-rate rise and fall. This is probably not good; I don't want her to find me mid-coronary or having a stroke! Calm down, just chill, she'll soon be here.

We were both in that difficult third year at university when we met. Exams were pressing; essays were mounting, and the realities of real life in the big wide world appearing on the horizon. We shared hours, evenings, nights and then days together. Sometimes we were hard to separate. We even went home to meet each other's parents. Hers in Cambridgeshire, mine in Leeds. I remember how gentle and soft her body was; delicate, fragile, but so responsive, so passionate, and so accepting of every touch. The others were different. Or maybe I was when I was with them. I could still remember making that silly pact with Danielle on graduation day, that if we were both alone and older, we'd be each other's standby husband or wife. That was, of course, before I met Jane. Oh, god, I fell in love with Jane, so very much in love. It was like something from a film, but played out for real, in real time, and with no regrets.

Jane and I met on a train. I was on my way to London for an interview with that advertising agency, the first one I worked for. She was going to visit her sister, who'd just had a baby. She sat in a table seat, facing the front. I'd booked the seat opposite, it turned out. I had to ask her to move her bag so I could get my feet under the table. I remember how our legs kept touching no matter how hard we tried to stop it happening. We both laughed about it and started to chat. When she went to the loo I wrote my name and number on a piece of paper and tucked it inside her coat pocket. I still remember her short dark hair and those heavily made up eyes, mascara weighing down her delicate lashes; the deep red lipstick. And that top barely covering her beautiful breasts. No bra underneath, her nipples were pushing discreetly against the cotton; inviting, alluring and tempting.

We met again two weeks later. To my surprise, she phoned me. I can still remember what she said:

"I'm the girl from the train, the one in the top you couldn't take your eyes off!"

"God, was I that obvious?" I remember saying back.

You're a man!" But then she laughed and added, "I was flattered." Her voice was so full of promise, so keen, so enthusiastic. I could hear her smile over the phone.

When we saw each other again we met as friends but parted as lovers. As she walked through the door we kissed each other's cheeks; when she left we kissed each other's lips. Between arriving and departing we exchanged life stories, preferences, loves, hopes, aspirations and dreams. We held hands. We kissed; we kissed again, more deeply. I touched her neck; she pulled off her top. Still no bra. I gently kissed, licked and felt her breasts. Soon the tension built and a tide of lust overwhelmed us. Clothes slid to the floor. The bed took our weight, the springs responding to our every move. We sweated, we rolled, we giggled and we swam through the sheets in that passion powered night. We snatched sleep in short reluctant bursts, just enough to relax and restore bodies that were desperate to be joined again. Afterwards I watched her dozing, a smile creeping over her lips, make up smudged and hair ruffled and soft. I still remember how we laughed as we staggered to the shower in the morning, sated by the passion of the night.

She was reluctant to leave. As we hugged goodbye she hung on to me, arms wound around my neck, desperate not to say goodbye. The chilly, post-dawn light dragged us both back to reality. But after that there was no real going back for either of us. She was the one, I knew. Within a month we were living together. Every kiss was special. It was as if together we'd invented sex. We seemed to wear each other on our sleeves, walking arm in arm, touching whenever we could, just to show the world we had something special, something new, something so good.

A year later we married in a register office, in front of lots of friends, and passed a dull celebratory afternoon with aged relatives. The honeymoon was special, though. A week in France in a tent! To be so happy together was lovely, and it would never end. Or so we thought.

Two daughters came along within a few years, lovely girls who were the image of their mother. They're both following her into teaching too. We moved house three times, each one bigger and better than the last. I became a partner in the agency. I was working long, late days but it seemed worth it when I had Jane to come home to. Then, out of nowhere, the shutters came down on our perfect life together. It's hard to remember it in this sunny, beautiful place. It's still so painful even six years on.

We were driving back from holiday. We'd been away on our own; the girls were in their late teens, one already at university and the other about to go. We'd landed at Gatwick, having flown in from Spain. We picked up the car from among the rows of vehicles where we had left it two weeks ago. We called the girls to say we'd cleared Customs and would be home in a few hours as planned. We drove off into the night, our minds already busy with thoughts of work the next morning and wondering what mail might be lying in wait for us at home.

Then it happened. Without warning. BANG. A big bang. Followed by silence. A horrible, nasty, evil silence. It never leaves you, you know, an experience like that. It haunts you in the night, in the cold, deep dark before dawn. The kid driving the other car was uninsured; no MOT and no tax. Jane died at the scene while I held her hand. I felt her fingers go limp. The boy racer ran away and fell into a ditch where he was picked up and arrested some minutes later. I was in a daze, numb, and unable to speak. I wished I'd died there too, just to be with her and not alone. I kept calling her name, telling her I loved her, begging her not to leave me. She was gone, though, empty. Her jaw was hanging open at an unnatural angle. There was blood on her face and her eyes were dull. The ambulance crew had to prise me away. In A & E I had a check-up. Afterwards I was sedated and taken home.

The bastard who killed her got a pitifully short sentence in a young offenders' institute. I got life, the rest of my life to be spent without Jane. Our daughters lost their mother. I spent the following hours, days and weeks wondering whether to end it all. How could I live without her? It was so unfair, what had she done to deserve this? I survived, of course. I crawled through the depths and edged my way up the sides of the pit of depression, to the glimmer of sunrise above. I think watching a young bird take flight for the first time made me realise that life continues, life always will continue, and our daughters would carry on her DNA to another generation. Jane would live on in our memories and maybe one day in future grandchildren.

Five and a half years later I went to one of those dreadful university reunions. Dreadful because you see all those

"Gosh, aren't I doing well?" people, who not only want to relate in detail how brilliantly they've done in life, but also how their little darling has

"Just reached grade eight on the Appalachian nose flute" and will soon be performing at some uninspiring, heavily subsidised concert, where the audience will be outnumbered by the musicians on stage.

You spend hours clutching glasses of cheap Chardonnay, asking and answering the inevitable "Whatever happened to...?" questions.

"Where's Danielle? What's she doing?" I asked her former room-mate. Karen told me she was still in touch with Danielle and that they met up every few months. I remember smiling and nodding as I learned she was a clinical shrink at a health centre in the Midlands. I was pleased for her. She'd married, had a daughter, but tragically her husband had died of cancer eighteen months before. So then I told Karen how my Jane had died.

She touched my arm and told me she was sorry. It was the same response as everyone gave. They all meant well, but they were powerless to bring her back. Fighting the sadness, I moved on and spoke to others, some I knew, some I didn't even recognise. We had all been fresh young students once. Now we were world-weary adults, carrying the baggage of our daily lives and the echoes of our individual history.

The campus looked similar to the way it had in my time. There were some new buildings but the atmosphere felt the same. I walked the familiar footpaths and more memories flooded back; some were welcome, others less so. That night I was back in a university room. Most of the people at the reunion were staying over. After the evening drinks do and the meal, we had talked ourselves hoarse and it was time to drift away. Some went into huddles, some even ended up sharing beds, recapturing their lost youth. I made my excuses and slipped away, found my room and went to bed. Wow, students had it good these days. The room had an en-suite! Mine used to be in a utilitarian block, with one bathroom between ten.

I fell asleep that night staring at the outside security light creeping past the badly fitting curtains. I found myself playing out in my mind those days here on the campus with Danielle. It was the first time I'd thought of any other woman apart from Jane.

A month later I was sitting in my office. Across my desk-top screen I gazed down at people walking in the street below. On the desk I saw Jane's photograph smiling back at me. It was one of the last pictures I'd ever taken of her, on that holiday a few days before she died. No, she didn't just "die", she was killed. Ripped from life by a useless, uncaring, selfish bastard who by now was probably back on the streets, probably driving illegally again and almost certainly having fun. All I had were my memories and a huge void in my heart. I don't know why but I decided to search for Danielle. After I'd typed in her name and the health area where she worked, up came her details on a staff list. She was the senior person there.

I started writing an email, then walked away, went outside, paced about in the rain and got very wet. I didn't notice. I walked into a coffee shop and ordered a cappuccino. I sat clutching it until it went cold. Back in the office my assistant called over and said there were a few calls for me to return. I nodded and smiled. I remember re-opening the half-written email and deciding to continue with it. It was difficult. Finally I wrote:

Danielle, hi, hope you remember me. I'm sorry to hear about your husband's early death. I lost my wife too so I know what it's like.

I went on with small, everyday ramblings about life, the universe and whatever else I could think of. Hit send and sat back.

Next morning when I picked up my phone I saw there was an email in my inbox from Danielle. I could hardly bring myself to open it in case it said something I didn't want to read. She said she sympathised with me in my loss. Then she told me about her life, her daughter and her husband's death. The scars never heal from such unimaginable pain, only slowly fade. At least she'd had a chance to say goodbye. I didn't have that with Jane.

Danielle signed off with a memory of graduation day and our waving goodbye. Was she inviting me to remember our pledge?

That night I went to where I'd scattered Jane's ashes. Under a tree, on a country riverside walk we used to enjoy. I sat on the soft, damp ground and almost asked her if she minded me contacting Danielle again. What a pointless, pitiful thing to do! Jane was no longer there. The only place she existed was in my memory and in the minds of our daughters, family and friends.

Back home I looked through the photographs, the early ones where we were overwhelmingly happy. Pictures which were taken to send as postcards to our futures, although we didn't realise how those futures would play out. If we had, we'd have enjoyed and lived more every day. Stupid rows would have been averted or walked away from; we wouldn't have wasted a single moment being anything other than loving to each other. I cried. I drank almost an entire bottle of wine and then I fell asleep on the sofa, clutching the photograph album that was all I had left of the days of happiness. Why, I thought, do we never tell the ones we love just how much they mean to us? Why do we live as if life will last forever, wasting days, wasting hours, wasting moments of precious life.

So here I am in Greece, sitting at a taverna table, bathed in womb-warm sunshine, waiting for the ferry to arrive and tie up.

Danielle and I emailed and phoned and eventually we met. We arranged to travel somewhere midway between our homes. We picked lunchtime, on a cold winter's Thursday. We sent each other photographs so we would know who to look out for, as if we could ever forget. I wore a casual jacket and a new shirt. I arrived early and grabbed a table in the little café we'd arranged to meet in, one plucked from an online map. She was late. Fifteen long, cruel minutes crawled past. Then I sighed in relief and my pulse began to quicken. I saw her crossing the street, it was unmistakably Danielle.

She still had that purposeful walk, that air of positivity I'd always associated her with. I got up and she saw me. She stopped in front of me, smiled and then sighed, her shoulders relaxing. She opened her arms and we went to hug, but instead she kissed me full on the lips, like a lover. For a moment time seemed to tilt sideways. For years I had kissed only Jane, but once there had been Danielle and that kiss had taken me back to our days together.

We both sat down and I ordered coffee and food. Neither of us ate much, though. We picked at it and chatted, talking fast and furious, like giggling schoolgirls do the morning after the night before. We poured out our histories, hopes and regrets. Then I brought up the pledge we'd made at graduation, the pledge that we'd be each other's standby husband and standby wife.

I was so scared she'd laugh it off or just reject the idea. I remember saying to her:

"Remember our graduation day promise?" and then touching her hand with my trembling fingers.

"Yes, of course, I do, Steve," she replied, smiling. I could see tears welling in her eyes. Could feel them in mine too.

"So," I remember saying, smiling back at her and holding her hand tight, desperate not to let the moment go,

"Here we are. Both of us left on our own. Danielle, do you need a standby husband?"

We both had tears running down our cheeks by then. We couldn't speak about it any further that day, we just hugged and then we both cried. I guess we were sharing grief and joy. We understood each other's loss; we felt we were safe with someone we could trust. The waiter asked if we were OK and brought us some tissues. We laughed it off and mumbled that we were fine, really, absolutely fine, thanks.

Danielle fumbled open the plastic wrapping and pulled out a tissue to wipe her eyes with.

"Oh, no, I've smudged it now... my make-up. I spent hours on that too," she laughed ruefully.

"Danielle, hey, you look fantastic," I assured her. "A bit of smudged make up doesn't worry me, it's you I want to see, in any state."

"Steve, you're so sweet, but I'm not a naive student any more, you know. I've had two children for one thing. Look, it's a lovely dream but I'm not sure I can do the relationship thing again... not the full on, falling in love and living together thing. God, it would be easy, though, especially with someone as gentle and lovely as you. You know, I often wondered if we should have stayed together, back then. But, hey, you never know how the road will turn, do you?"

She didn't say no outright, though, and from that I had drawn hope.

I remember feeling desperate to make it work. I felt that it could, if only Danielle would agree to give it a go. We let ourselves dream out loud, talking possibilities and practicalities; we had two homes, two jobs, and between us three almost grown-up children. Well, mostly grown up, truth be told. None of this was insurmountable if we really wanted to make it work. There was no rush, after all.

Danielle's daughter, though, was still devastated by her father's death and had begged her mother never to allow another man to replace him. She was being treated for depression and had just split up from her long-term boyfriend, the one she'd had since school. She was now nineteen, at university, but still desperately badly hit by the loss of her father even though he had died a few years ago.

Could Danielle persuade her daughter that she needed a new direction in life now? While she'd always love the man she'd married, that man was now gone and she needed more than mourning, wishing and remembering.

When I told my girls what we were considering, I was amazed by their response. They both hugged me and said,

"Go for it, Dad!"

But would Danielle let herself believe that we could do this together? How I hoped she would. After our reunion lunch I asked, almost desperately:

"Danielle, will you consider it?"

And she gave me an honest reply.

"Look, Steve, I may not be able to have a proper relationship with you. I may never be able to sleep with you in the same bed. We could share a room, but maybe sex is never going to happen for us. I just don't know. I still fancy you, don't get me wrong, but you're going to have to give me time, maybe even a lifetime."

I told her then,

"Take all the time you need. And if it never happens, at least I have the memories of what we shared in the past. Just being with you would be enough for me, sharing the happy times and supporting each other through the bad ones."

We parted then after a long hug and I went home. For the first time in six years I felt hopeful. Maybe the life ahead of me was still worth living, or it would be if Danielle felt the same way.

We chatted on the phone a week after that and decided we'd wait to meet up again, but that when we did, we'd do so in a romantic, beautiful place with no associations for either of us.

Weeks went by. Then a month, then two, and it was becoming clear that we both had doubts. It's one thing being lovers as young adults, just hatched into life, embracing the joy of living, with taut, perfect bodies and heads full of brand new dreams. It's another carrying the sadness and baggage of loss; the scars that come with age and experience.

The prospect of getting to know someone intimately again is daunting for both of us. Are we anything like the two people we once were? Still, "The Child is Father of the man" and all that. I guess we are the same in many ways, we're just older. But what if we suddenly find we have opposing views about important things? Different tastes? Habits that irritate and annoy? Oh, bugger, then I guess we try to accommodate each other and accustom ourselves and respond accordingly. Easier said than done, but no one ever said love was simple. Maybe that's why so many relationships break down. Partners suddenly stop making allowances, trying to accommodate the other and to make things work. That's why the loss of my wife and Danielle's husband is doubly hard, because it seems we both had great marriages.

There is no guarantee if we do get together that it will last. We might just limp along. Or maybe it will be as glorious as we both want our new relationship to be. But what if she decides to commit herself and then we're incompatible in bed? I guess we just start from the basics and anything else is a bonus. After visiting the darkest depths, having her company on any level would feel so good to me.

Three months after that lunchtime meeting we agreed to meet up here, on the island. I said I'd book accommodation and then we would give it a go. Two single beds in a double room, just sleeping together in the same place, in separate beds. No expectations, no demands, absolutely no pressure. I told her we could have the lights off to get undressed and I'd leave the room to give her space whenever she needed it. Even holding hands in the dark with someone in the next bed would be wonderful.

But I can't help wondering: if it does feel right for both of us, will we have sex on the first night? We did when we first met all those years ago.

I fear though, for good or bad, I'll dive in head-first and fall madly in love with her all over again. I think actually I already am in love with her. I've been thinking of nothing else but Danielle since I booked the flight. Every week that went by without her confirming we'd do this trip has been torture to me. Even after she agreed and said she'd booked her flight, I hardly dared to believe it. The turning point was when she sent me an email late one night. The subject was "My daughter". I was terrified to open it in case it read:

After hours of discussion I have to accept that my daughter is still too upset by the idea of my being with someone else...

Instead Danielle had written:

My daughter has finally said she's OK with the idea of my being with someone else...

I read it, I read it again and then I cried. I actually fell asleep on the settee with my phone in my hand, the email still displayed.

So now here we are. I arrived yesterday evening and checked in to the hotel. Yannis the owner seems charming, and the rooms are lovely. It's small and well-kept. I did, though, receive one dreadful shock. After taking my bag up to the room and unpacking, I came back down to the lobby where Yannis was waiting to check that everything was all right.

"Any messages for you will be left in the pigeon hole with your room number," he explained.

I smiled and glanced over. My heart skipped a beat as I grabbed a piece of paper and unfolded it. I stared in disbelief at the message:

Sorry, can't come after all. Big work issues.

I was flooded with panic. Then I forced myself to look again and realised the message was from "Dan". Now Danielle is always Danielle, never Dan or Danny. Then I looked back at the row of pigeon holes and realised the one designated for our room was above the key and not below it. There was nothing in that box. I'd simply read a message intended for someone else. Or had I?

That's when I texted Danielle to ask if she was OK and instantly received a reply: *Just boarding!*

No wonder my heart keeps racing. She'll love it here. There are lemon trees in the hotel garden bursting with fruit, and figs growing nearby too. We've got a room overlooking the bay, with a little balcony shaded by bougainvillaea. The deep red flowers glowing against the white-painted walls. There are swallows darting about above and the scent of wild herbs fills the air. I can hear the serenade of cicadas from the tree-covered hill above, and below in the bay yachts come and go. It is an Idyllic setting.

In a few hours we will know where we stand. Maybe we will just share the room as friends. We could decide just to enjoy a holiday together and then part for the final time. Or perhaps we will meet like lovers reunited, ready to make love like we did when we first met; sometimes in need, sometimes in lust, always in love.

If it does go well, we'll decide whether or not to move in together or even to get married. The kids are all onside now and they say they're happy for us whatever we decide. They seem to think, though, that it's now a foregone conclusion and that we will become an item. Hey, I'm getting ahead of myself. There's a lot to play out before I even dare hope for that.

Oh, it's here! I didn't notice it coming round the headland. The little ferry is already docking, pumping out clouds of black diesel exhaust as it maneuvers alongside the quay and ties up. Yes, it's Danielle's ferry. She'll be walking off it now. If I stand up and wave she'll see me... there she is, she's waving back. Oh, I love that hat! It's just so her, and that dress... Diaphanous, delicate and warm, brightening her lovely long legs. Oh, god, she is something else. Keep calm, just wait.

Here she comes. Careful, mustn't knock over the coffee cup as I stand up. Mustn't appear desperate to see her. Oh, sod that!

"Danielle! How wonderful to see you in this... well, wonderful place."

"Hi, Steve. Lovely to see you too. This is beautiful, what a great place! It's so much prettier than in the photographs. How's the hotel?"

"Oh, you'll love it. It's just up there, on the right… see the bougainvillaea over our balcony?"

"Steve, I think I'm OK with this, but please don't expect too much, will you? Don't hurt me, but above all don't turn me away."

"I'll be your standby husband if you'll be my standby wife. Hey! Listen… it's an omen."

On the taverna's music system we can hear a familiar song: The Pretenders' "I'll Stand By You".

"Sorry, Danielle, for crying like this. You must think I'm bonkers," I say.

"Steve, if you're bonkers then so am I."

Danielle is wiping away tears as she speaks.

I open my arms to her. We just stare into each other's waiting, begging eyes.

"My standby wife, let's just hold each other, and never, ever let go," I say.

The waiter, watching from behind the taverna bar, turned up the music that seemed to have had such an effect on his customers, now busily laughing and talking and hoping together.

He poured a couple of glasses of ouzo. These would be on the house.

Broken Bikini

The waiter at the taverna by the water took over two drinks to the table by the sea. A woman in her mid-thirties sat on a cushioned wicker chair with a view over the bay. Opposite her sat a younger man, in his late twenties at a guess. He had sun-bleached hair, a deep tan, a small tattoo on his shoulder. He was smiling at his companion. The woman took a long sip of her drink, looked down and then up again, and started to speak to him. The waiter discreetly listened as he took his time walking back to the bar.

"So, look, Daniel, I wanted you to come and meet me here because things have changed for me... changed in ways I could never have imagined. It's been a bit of a shock... no, a hell of a shock. But now I'm able to make some big decisions and they involve you, I hope."

"Just listen and don't say anything, if you don't mind. It's going to take a while, and I might not get through this without breaking down so be warned. It involves some amazing revelations and things which will shock you about me. About what I've done, what's been done to me, I guess about who I really am. I'm still coming to terms with a lot of it myself.

Let's go back to where things started. Last year, right, when I was out here on a flotilla sailing holiday with my friend Rachel, and you were the lead skipper. I was instantly attracted to you, and I may be ten years older but I knew straight away that you liked me too.

I want to apologise to you now for seducing you and then turning you away. There were reasons why I acted like that, reasons I hope you'll soon understand. I couldn't tell you much about myself then, or where my head was at, because I'd recently suffered a bereavement and wasn't thinking straight.

OK, look, I didn't tell you this then, but I didn't just fancy you, I *really* fancied you, and I know you were keen on me too. Well, at least, I thought you were... no, don't answer, I can tell by your expression that you were. I hope you still are.

Do you know how much self-control it took for me not to kiss you that first night of the holiday, when we were walking along the cliff top track above the little bay on Meganissi? You took me right to the end, to show me the lights of the mainland opposite.

I really wanted you then. I wanted to have sex with you, right there in the early-evening light, but I just... well, for lots of reasons, I didn't. I didn't tell you about myself either, did I? I found out about you, though. That you were a few years out of university; had drifted into sailing and then become a yacht master, lead skipper for that holiday firm. A free spirit. I liked that. It's why I had my moment of weakness."

"Rachel said I was losing it when I told her I wanted you. It was the day we'd moored up the flotilla in that small port on Ithaca. You came aboard to see if we were OK and I invited you in. Rachel made an excuse and left. I knew it was wrong but I had to kiss you then, I had to hold you. There was just something about you… Afterwards I felt awful, as if I'd just been using you; we'd had sex, and then I asked you to leave.

No, it wasn't just sex. We made love. I felt it was really special, seriously, so much better than my recent relationships had been. You were so caring, so tender, but I was annoyed with myself. You see, back home I'd just begun a relationship. I felt I'd behaved appallingly. I'd two-timed someone once before… well; I'll come to that in a moment. You'll probably think I'm a real slut when I've finished. But maybe you'll see the real me and the reasons why I've done what I've done."

"My own guilt at two-timing Jason was the reason why I turned you away the next night, and the nights after that, though I kept wanting you, kept spending time with you. It must have seemed like I was leading you on, kissing you, touching you, and then stopping and backing off. I'm so sorry. You deserved better than that, or at least an explanation."

"Look, can we hold hands, please? Thanks. Oh, I'm not sure that I'll be able to tell you all I want to but… oh, listen, Dan, they're playing one of my Mum's favourite songs! Steve Harley, 'The Best Years of our Lives'. Hey, it could be, you know, this could be the best year of my life. Maybe. Sorry, I'd better carry on.

"I didn't tell you this before but I was brought up by my Mum in a commune in Essex. It was in a big, old rambling house in ten acres of land where we raised goats, chickens and dope plants. Yup, lots of those. I remember open fires and the smell of wood smoke, and also the damp, and the cold bedrooms. The windows didn't fit and the wind howled in. The house was scary too, especially at night. Most of the people there were really nice, and I loved growing up with lots of other kids. Running around the grounds, free, happy and healthy. We never seemed to need doctors.

It didn't last, though. When I was eight the commune closed down. There was some scandal… well, a big one really. The drugs stuff got more intense, and there was a death. A woman drowned in the pond while she was stoned. She was my mum's best friend. It hit Mum badly, but it made her get a grip and forced her to reassess her life. She realised that it could so easily have been she who'd died. It's funny how a death makes you think about where you are, where you're going, what you're doing with your life.

Social Services took away the dead woman's children and they were adopted, I think, or maybe they went to live with a relative. Anyway the commune fell apart. Mum stopped calling herself Magnolia and reverted to her real name, Jennifer.

"She had grown up in France. Her parents were both artists, quite well-known ones too, they lived in the Charente near Cognac and ran painting courses. They offered Mum and me a home there but Mum wanted to stay in the UK. She was a fluent French speaker, and although she never had any formal teaching qualification she got a job teaching French at a small private school near London. We moved into a rented cottage in a village close by. I went to the local school and life was OK really, but Mum was always distant and never spoke much about the past.

A year or so later I went to high school and then on to a nearby art college. I loved it, found myself discovering talents I'd never guessed I had. They must have come from my grandparents. I loved life drawing, the differences between the models. Some perfection, others just humdrum, but all real people.

"Inevitably it was there I fell in love, with another first-year student. Mark was my first proper boyfriend. He had a bedsit and we went there after college and had sex, lots of sex. Good sex, exciting sex, fresh boyfriend and new girlfriend sex. We thought it would never end, we thought we would spend eternity together and be artists like my grandparents, living the dream and becoming famous, our pictures adorning the walls of the rich and famous. Each night would last for ever, and each morning was a wonderful way to start the day. It was as if we'd invented kissing, discovered love and found sex like no one ever had before. The naivety of youth, hey?

"Then I met Rod. I saw him on-stage in a pub in the town; he was a guitarist and singer. I thought his words and music were magical. I felt myself being drawn to him more and more. I asked Mark to take me to one of his gigs. We went to a couple of them and at one I spoke to Rod when he'd come off-stage and told him how much I liked his music. It must have been obvious that I fancied him; obvious to him and obvious to my boyfriend. Mark was really uncomfortable. I think he knew where it was going to lead.

"A few days later I saw Rod's name on a chalkboard outside a small club and I went to meet him on my own. I hadn't told Mark, just said I was going out, but he suspected something as I'd dressed up and washed my hair. I said I'd be back later. The gig was as good as the others, and I made sure Rod saw me in the front row of the audience. After he'd finished playing he bought me a drink, and then suggested we got a takeaway. We went back to his place, a ground-floor flat in a large Victorian house.

"We ate, we drank, and we smoked some dope. Why I'm not sure. I'd hardly touched the stuff before because of Mum's friend, but he offered it to me and I accepted. I felt myself drifting in and out of a haze. I remember him kissing me, and then slowly undoing the buttons on the front of my dress. Soon it was off my shoulders and my breasts were on show. I wasn't wearing a bra; I didn't much in those days. He slipped his hand inside my pants and I just fell back, letting him do whatever he wanted. I stayed the night, and we had sex, and then we did it again in the morning. I was glowing, I loved it. I'd seduced this cool musician. My happiness, though, would be short-lived.

"Later that day I saw Mark in college and he knew. He told me to get my stuff, move out of his bedsit and leave him alone. I cried, I'd thrown away Mark, but I thought I'd got Rod. Except it turned out that I didn't. That evening I went to his door and knocked on it, standing there like Little Miss Lost, all my possessions in a rucksack and a small case. He opened the door, but behind him was a woman; they were just on their way out. She was older than me, sophisticated, pretty.

"He said, 'Oh, hi. Hey, good to see you last night! Sorry I can't be of more help. Oh, by the way, this is my girlfriend Trish. We're just off. I've got a gig in town. See you around sometime.' "I'd been picked up, screwed and cast aside. I spent the evening touring round various girlfriends trying to find somewhere to stay for a few days, and luckily one of them had a spare sofa.

"A few weeks later I was invited to do some life modelling by one of the lecturers. He was my favourite teacher at the college so I was keen to impress him. He told me it was for a private life drawing class and it would be held at his house. There was money in it as well, so I agreed.

I went along and it was all quite proper, held in the sitting room of a nice Georgian house. There was a mixed group of three artists plus the lecturer. Two of the three were women; the other was an older man. I was shown into a room where I could undress and there was a gown for me to put on. I walked back into the room and took off the dressing gown just before I sat on the chair. It was all fine, very ordinary, quite relaxed. I was asked back and it became a regular thing. It was a good arrangement as it meant money for me and a model for them.

"Then on the fourth occasion the tutor, Simon, said he was totally out of order but he really liked me, and if I wasn't one of his students, and if he was ten years younger, he'd ask me out. I shrugged. Feeling in need of affection, I said I would be honoured to be asked out, and I wasn't going to tell anyone if he wasn't. Besides, I really liked Simon. He was kind, fun, had a spirit of adventure, and there were photographs all over his walls of the places he'd been to and the things that he'd done.

"He had one thing in common with my mum as well. His favourite band was Broken Bikini and there was a picture of them on his bedroom wall, with the lead guitarist, Bridges Brody, on the very edge of the stage, leaning out over the audience in a classic rock pose. Mum loved them. She was such a fan! So we went out together, Simon and I. Being forbidden made it more thrilling and soon I sneakily moved in with him. He was single, and so long as no one knew, it was fine. It wasn't illegal, I was over eighteen; it just wasn't great for a tutor to be having sex with a student.

We'd drive to college together and I'd leap out half a mile before the building, arriving after him, having walked the last bit of the journey. I sat in classes he was taking and smugly knew I'd be sleeping with our lecturer later that night.

"So I finished the course, left college and sort of drifted. I was still living with Simon, and he wasn't asking for any rent or food money so it all seemed good. I went to see my mum and while I was there I found out the school she taught at needed an art assistant. I applied for the job and they gave it to me. Being a private school they could take on anyone they wanted, of course. I was fresh out of Art College and keen, and I was closer to the age of most of the kids there than the other members of staff were, so it worked for all of us. It was agreed I could start mid-way through the term, which I did. I bought a small moped to commute between school and Simon's house.

"He and I were good together. He went to the college and taught during the day, while I went to my mum's school and also taught. They'd basically got another art teacher on the cheap. Still, after a few months the regular art teacher went on maternity leave and I got to fill in for her, for a bit more money, so it worked out OK. Of course it went downhill from there and I came down to earth with a shocking great bump, as you're about to hear.

"Most Thursday nights I'd still model at Simon's house for his life drawing classes. It was no big deal and I enjoyed seeing their work. I loved the way some people tried to draw my tattoo, the one on the top of my arm and shoulder. It's unique… well, almost. My mum had the same one, but I've never seen anything else like it. She had a tattooist in town copy it for me one day when I asked if I could have it done. I was just eighteen. She'd originally had it created after a festival where Broken Bikini were topping the bill on their first tour. The design is her interpretation of one of their album covers. After this particular drawing class, when the artists had gone home, Simon asked if I would model for photographs too. I wasn't that keen but he said it could make us money. There was very little cash in life drawing classes with the amateur artists, but photography… well, people would pay well for a pretty model like me. Simon told me he was also a bit concerned because the spectre of cuts had come up at the college and he was in danger of losing his job. I said I'd think about it, but he pushed me about it in quite a forceful way. I eventually said that I'd try it, and that weekend, on the Friday night, ten men turned up.

"They weren't like the drawing class artists, they were more ordinary. Big lenses, loads of kit, lots of chat about effects, and black and white over colour, and so on. I'd done a bit of photography as part of my course and I knew how to use f-stops and film speeds, and about framing, focus, and lightness and brightness, but I was no expert. So they set up their tripods and cameras. Simon had erected a white backdrop behind the wooden chair, the one I sat on for the life drawing classes. Then I was handed a couple of dresses one of the photographers had brought along for me to wear. They weren't my style at all, but I was happy to put them on even though they were tight and a bit ill-fitting. I walked back into the room.

"While I'd been changing they'd set up proper lights, so I posed in the first dress, then I went off and changed into the second one. I thought,

This is OK, no worries here. How wrong I was. Simon came over to me and said he wanted me to wear a basque. Straight out, just like that, and he gave me a package containing a red and black lacy corset. I said I felt a bit uncomfortable with that, as it had suddenly gone from art to glamour in the blink of an eye. He just said: 'Yes, that's why they're here. They've paid £35 each for a glamour model session.' While I listened with my mouth open and my throat going dry, he reminded me that as there were ten of them it worked out at £350 in all and they'd already paid. He also reminded me I hadn't given him anything towards food or accommodation, and pointed out that I was hardly in a position to back out now. I didn't say anything. I felt trapped and very uncomfortable, but I put it on, the basque. I walked back into the room feeling like a stripper, and saw the waiting pack... because that's what I felt they were... all leering eyes, fat sweaty fingers and flesh-hungry lenses, desperate to capture me in the skimpy underwear. It was degrading.

"I posed on the chair as the camera shutters clicked. Soon, of course, they wanted more flesh and it wasn't long before Simon had persuaded me to be topless and then nude. Now normally I didn't mind that when I posed for the life classes, but this seemed to be different. To these guys breasts were just tits. The poses I was asked for became more explicit. They wanted open-leg shots, and more. I did a couple then I ran off, in tears.

"Simon came after me. Instead of doing what a supportive, loving boyfriend should have done, hugging me and saying he was sorry, and that it had all gone too far, he gripped my shoulder forcefully, his fingers leaving red marks. He said I needed to 'get a grip' as they'd paid money, and if I carried on they might even pay more. He told me if I refused I might as well move out. I was all alone and being threatened with eviction.

I dried my eyes and meekly walked back into the room where the men were waiting, with their piercing eyes and dirty minds. I just did what Simon said, even when he handed me a sex toy. I sat there with my legs open, displaying myself as their lenses got closer and the lights burned my eyes. I tried to think of nice things as a distraction but I felt more and more betrayed, very vulnerable, and completely used and abused.

"As soon as they'd gone I got dressed and walked outside. Simon had told them as they left that there would be another session 'same time next week', and it was then I realised that I had to get out of this, and fast. What would they want next time?"

"I got on to my moped and drove to Mum's. I told her what had happened but she wasn't too shocked. She said I was right to get out, with the way it was going. What was going to happen to those pictures? I thought. Pictures of me exposed like that? What would Simon want next? A proper porn film?

"The next day I took the afternoon off work claiming a doctor's appointment, and while Simon was at college I went to his house and packed my stuff. I got a taxi back to Mum's.

It was the day after that when she told me she was giving up her job and moving to France to live with my grandparents. They were both ill and Granddad was suffering from a bad heart condition. Mum was really quite depressed, I could tell. Luckily I was able to take over renting her cottage.

"The school wanted me to stay on, and they offered me a full teacher's salary. I accepted. I didn't see Simon again after that, but I'm sure he soon got a new, keen young student to be his nude model and live-in girlfriend. She was welcome to him.

"A few years later both my grandparents were dead and Mum was in a bad way. My grandfather had died first but Gran followed him a few months later after catching pneumonia. I went to France for the funeral. All the local people came; my gran had been well liked over there. It had been their home for years and they were part of the community. Mum knew most of them quite well too; she'd grown up there after all. She didn't really recover from her depression, though. She became more and more withdrawn and eventually committed suicide. She took an overdose at the house in France. It was on the anniversary of the death of her best friend at the commune.

"Mum had very few friends left, but a couple of the old commune people turned up for her funeral, and there were a few colleagues from the school as well. Some of the old neighbours travelled from France, which was kind. We had a simple ceremony at the local crematorium, and as I said goodbye to everyone I realised I was now completely alone. I found myself feeling depressed too, and began to worry what my future was going to be.

"I guess I was emotionally vulnerable at the time, but I allowed myself to be chatted up by Jason, the young solicitor who'd been handling my mum's estate. The French house was a problem and could easily have become a nightmare. I decided to rent it out and happily a young couple from the same village moved in. It gave me an income and helped me live rather than just exist on my teacher's salary, as the cottage was really expensive to rent. I let Jason take me out for a curry. He was OK, charming even. We sort of fell into a relationship.

"I guess I was just too relaxed about it, the ultimate easy lay, too casual for my own good. That's why I liked you, Daniel. I know you'd have responded if I'd made a move on you that first night of the holiday, but you didn't push, and even when I seduced you, you let me take the lead and didn't go further than I was comfortable with at any time. Thank you. Jason wasn't like that. He kind of expected it, expected me to offer myself to him. We ended up in bed after that first meal and it sort of became a habit. We'd go out, he'd buy a meal, and then we'd go back to his house and go straight to bed.

"A couple of weeks after that first night with him I came out here to Greece for the sailing holiday and that's when I met you. I told Jason I needed time to escape and take stock after Mum's death, and the will and everything, and that I would be back afterwards. Sadly I was back with him too. I went home and felt really low. Jason was solid, but dull and dependable. I felt I needed that, though, as I myself was neither confident nor positive. I ended up on anti-depressants. Jason introduced me to his friends and eventually I moved in with him. It just sort of became a default position, as they say. It wasn't that bad at first. Just, well, convenient, and I guess it gave me someone to talk to, someone to be with.

"Months later I was going through Mum's stuff, the bits I'd brought back to Britain from the house in France, and I found out just how keen she'd been on Broken Bikini… you know, the rock band? She had all of their albums, photographs, old tickets, tour tee shirts, posters, the lot. One of the band had signed something for her too. It was a ticket to a show of theirs and it had some lovely words on it. Mum had had it framed. It read: *Great gigs, great nights, Stella times! Always, Bridges xx*

It was in a bag with a lock of my hair from when I was a baby, and an old photograph of her friend from the commune. It was all that was left of a wasted life, I thought, a great talent left unused. Then I realised people probably thought the same about me as well, repeating my mother's mistakes and reliving her life. Withdrawing and going for the easiest option, allowing myself to be used, abused and walked over by the poor choices in men I'd made. Poor old Mark, the boyfriend I'd cheated on, was the best one I'd had, and I'd been so cruel to him by going off and sleeping with Rod. It must have gutted him. Well, it did, I know.

"I decided then to get a grip, and stop taking the pills. I asked Jason to take me to see Broken Bikini. They were doing a new tour, the first for some years, it was a sort of comeback, and they had a new album out as well. He was dismissive and said they just weren't his thing, he didn't like guitar bands and that was that. We rowed about it but it was important to me. This was the one link I had to my mum's past and I wanted to enjoy the music that she'd enjoyed, to taste the atmosphere she'd experienced. He said he'd go if it was really that important to me, so I bought two tickets for their show in London.

"The evening of the show came and we travelled in on the train, and then queued outside the arena waiting to get in. Jason was moaning constantly, and I was beginning to wonder why I was with him. We lived together and shared a bed but we weren't even really good friends, just sort of house mates with sex, and not very good sex at that. Well, maybe good for him but not good enough for me. There was no passion, it was just routine.

"I had decided to embrace the spirit of the evening and was wearing my mum's old Broken Bikini tour tee shirt under a faded leather jacket of hers, with jeans. I grabbed Jason's hand and pulled him with me to the front. We shoved and twisted our way through the crowd and got to the barriers beneath the stage. I was really excited; I'd been listening to their music for weeks and quite liked them by then. Jason kept slagging them off, telling me they weren't the sort of thing he liked, and that I shouldn't like them either. What?!

"Eventually the band came on stage, and there was Bridges Brody, strutting out in denim and leather, guitar slung like a weapon over his hips, smiling face, hair still there, personality as big as the arena. Next to him was the singer. Tall, handsome, now shaven-headed but still looking fit and toned. The bassist, drummer and keyboard player joined them on stage, and then the lights built in intensity, flooding the stage; it was the build up to the opening number.

"There he was, my mum's dream man, Bridges Brody, standing a few feet away, just above me on the stage. His fingers lingered on the strings, and then it started. His hand rose as if in slow motion and thumped down, making those six metal strings vibrate.

"The first chords of the opening number caused the crowd to roar its approval. There was a surge of joy in everybody… Well, everyone, it seemed, except Jason. He shouted in my ear that he thought Bridges was out of tune and the singer was flat. It didn't put me off, though. I was loving it and also living it for Mum. I felt as if she was somewhere out there in the audience, almost with me. I could imagine her, here in the front row all those years ago, her head thrown back, hair tossing, make up glistening, singing along.

"The band played two sets with a short break in between. After the first, Jason suggested we should leave early:"It's not that good," he said, and added, "they ought to give this up and retire!"

"I told him he could go if he wanted, and that I would find my own way home. I was definitely staying for the second set. He just walked out and left. I stayed, and his place in the front row was quickly filled by other fans crushing forward for the second half. It was brilliant, even better than the first.

"After the encore I went to find the stage door. I wanted to get the ticket signed, sort of for Mum really. Sounds silly, I know. Then after forty minutes of waiting, cooling down with the sweat drying on my now smelly tee shirt, and after a few of the others had drifted off, the tour manager came to the door and said the band were really tired and could only spare us a few minutes. The other three people who'd been waiting with me were all women. They were Mum's age, and they wanted to see the singer. I asked to speak to Bridges. I wanted to show him the tour tee shirt and the signed ticket he'd given to Mum. I was ushered through."

"The well-lit auditorium gave way to the shabby, poorly lit back-stage corridor, and I was led to a dressing room a few metres away. There inside were the band themselves. Towels over their shoulders, wine bottles opened; sandwiches, crisps and numerous snacks littering a large table. The set list lying discarded in the bin."

"Bridges Brody still looked the part. They all did. He smiled at me, and I said: 'Hello, I'm here for my mum who was a huge fan. I wanted to show you this.' I offered up the signed ticket. He looked at it and then at me. He looked closely at my tee shirt, and I realised he was staring in particular at my arm, which had the top of the tattoo showing, the image of the band's first album cover. He looked at me again and asked me what my mum's name was. I said Jennifer; he shook his head as if to say he didn't remember her. Then it occurred to me, and I said: 'She was also known as Magnolia…'

"Bridges interrupted me there: 'Or, as I called her, Stella. As in Magnolia stellata, the star magnolia, the name of a pretty, small tree, because she was truly a star to me, a real star. I wrote that song on the second album about her: "Stella, You're a Star". It was a massive hit single, one of the biggest we had. It was the second encore we played tonight. I wrote on that old ticket you've got framed "Stella nights". That's what it meant.'

"Then it hit me. I knew that song. I knew the lyrics. Oh, god. It was gradually dawning on me. 'So my mum was… my mum… my mum was a groupie? The one in the song, that groupie? Your groupie?'

"There was an awkward silence. The other members of the band had stopped talking and were now openly looking at me and listening to our conversation."

"Bridges cleared his throat. 'At first,' he said, 'yes, she was. Er… sit down. I think I know who you are. Look, have some wine. Just let me just see that tattoo properly.'

"And with that he took hold of the bottom of my tee shirt and lifted it up. Luckily I was wearing a bra that night! I protested, 'Whoah, hang on!' But he said: 'Hey, it's not like that, believe me. This is important,' and lifted it up and off, fully exposing the tattoo on my arm and shoulder. I felt a bit silly, dressed in my white bra and jeans, holding Mum's old leather jacket in the middle of a group of sweaty musicians. 'There's only one tattoo like that,' he said, and smiled.

"Then he cleared his throat again, and with emotion building in his voice he told me: 'Your mum came backstage one night on the tour after we'd released our first album. Don't think badly of her… I took advantage of her, true enough, but it wasn't like the usual post-gig frolics. There was something between us, something special. I invited her to stick with us, and she travelled in the bus with me during the rest of the tour. She was just great fun. Look, back then, that was the way it was. I'm not going to apologise for anything.'

"'Hey,' I said, 'I'm not looking for an apology.' I put my tee shirt back on, trying to come to terms with this shock. My mum had been a groupie. Wow, I thought, that's actually a bit rock and roll!

"Bridges asked where she was and seemed very sad when I told him she was dead. He shook his head and told me it could have been different, but after the last night with my mum he'd taken up with the female singer of another band, the support act. I remember reading about him and the singer in a magazine cutting in my mum's stuff. It had been a big show biz relationship. It didn't last, of course. They were together for about ten years, I guess, and then they split up.

"I felt very close to Bridges then and gave him a hug. There was a strong smell of sweat when I held him to me, but I could feel him go weak in my arms. I'd never known that to happen before. All the men I'd been with apart from Mark were strong and tough, like I'd thought Bridges was. After all, this was Bridges Brody the 'axe man' from Broken Bikini! All denim and leather and loud guitars."

"'You know, she told me she'd had a baby, she wrote to me through the record company. She said she'd had a girl; that was you?' he asked, and added that his then girlfriend had thrown the letter away so he'd had no chance of writing back. 'Yes, there's only one of me so far as I know,' I half laughed as I replied.

'Then I think we might be father and daughter, kid.' He said, choking up.

"After a few seconds we allowed ourselves to accept that fact and Bridges hugged me. I broke down and cried. I was stunned. Was I really a groupie's daughter? Was this my father? I felt his closeness and realised it was probably true. I remembered my mum sitting alone at night listening to Broken Bikini, and singing their songs to me when I was young.

I felt my tee shirt, Mum's old tour tee shirt, getting wet again. Bridges was weeping on to my shoulder, crying over the memory of my mum and what might have been. He told me he'd been utterly stupid to have gone off with someone else and left Mum at the stage door. He said it was the biggest regret of his life.

"After an emotional two hours spent in that scruffy dressing room with Bridges after the rest of the band had gone, I went home. He insisted on paying for a cab for me all the way from London. He took my address and said he'd be in touch.

"So a month later we'd had DNA tests and, yes, there was no doubt really. My actual dad was Bridges – well, real name Nigel – Brody. Mum had been a real rock chick; I was conceived in the back of a tour bus after a sweaty gig, and my mum had ripped off her knickers for a bad boy guitar hero, probably watched by the rest of the band and their groupies too. Not the best start maybe but, hey, she'd had a song written about her. I also had a dad! A dad I knew, a dad I'd finally held and hugged, a dad who maybe even cared for me.

"When I got home Jason was up waiting for me. I was desperate to tell him my news, but he wouldn't let me speak. He seemed determined to utterly destroy me. He shouted at me, telling me I should have come back hours ago, and how dare I go backstage like a common groupie? He asked if I'd gone to 'screw that bloody guitarist'".

"I quietly replied that I would hardly have slept with my own father. I then told him how I'd finally found out who I was and how I'd met my dad. Jason went quiet and then he got really angry and shot me down again. He was not impressed that I was proud of my mum's past as a groupie. He said I should be ashamed of her instead, and if I was going to be the mother of his children I needed to get a clearer moral perspective. Whoah! I told him I wasn't ashamed of my mum, who was a child of her time. It wasn't as if she'd slept with lots of musicians from bands. It was, so far as I knew, only with him, Bridges Brody from Broken Bikini.

"I next met Bridges Brody in a very upmarket London restaurant a few days after the DNA tests had come through. He told me it was now confirmed that I was his daughter. He said he really wished things had been different. He and Mum had only spent a week together, and he hadn't realised at the time that those few days had been the key which should have unlocked a long and happy life together for them both; he just hadn't grasped the moment, and she'd felt unable to do so, because he was the star and she was a groupie. Between them they'd let their precious chance slip through their fingers and fade away forever. He also said I was his only child, and would be inheriting quite a bit of his estate one day. He promised me I need never be short of cash, and had already arranged for a large payment to be made into my bank account. This was incredibly generous and a huge relief as my job at the school had come to an end. He told me he wished my mum had contacted him again, after that one time she'd got a letter to him, to tell him she'd given birth to me and that I was his child.

"We said we'd get together soon and he'd show me his house... well, his estate, I guess. It's a big rambling pile in Surrey apparently. I did need a holiday first, though, and I told him I had something important to do. So I went home... well, back to Jason's, which had become my home. Things had been very strained between us but we were still together, just. I told him I'd been really pleased to meet my dad again, and how I'd recognised various personality traits we shared. Maybe I was just looking for some connection between us, but it seemed to be there nevertheless.

Jason though, was horrible again. He asked me how I could be pleased to be related to a 'yob', and said that Bridges was only my father because he'd screwed a 'slag' – in other words, my mother. He told me that she was 'worse than a whore' because, according to him, 'at least whores get paid'. He then added: 'And if you're going to be the mother of my children, you'd better get a grip on your morals and forget about him and his type.'

"I walked out. I booked into a hotel and went back to get my things the next day when I knew he was at work. I went into his office but his secretary said he was 'far too busy' to see me. So there in a room full of his clients, I said: 'Tell him his girlfriend, the daughter of a groupie who was worse than a whore, is going on holiday. I won't be answering his calls or texts, and I've moved out. Oh. And you can say that the last thing I'd ever do is let him father any child of mine. My standards are far too high for me to allow myself to be impregnated by a narrow-minded little tosser. I've dumped him. 'Bye.' I walked out, leaving her open-mouthed. Then I called my friend Rachel to see if she wanted to come out here to Greece with me again, but she was busy and couldn't get time off work. So I booked to come here on my own. I'm staying at the little hotel up there on the hillside. Yannis is a great hotelier, and this taverna… wow, it's perfect!

"Look, the reason I came back here to Greece, to this island, was to find you, Dan. I called the sailing company and they said you were now doing private charters for another firm, but they gave me the number. The woman in the office there said she'd get a message to you, and, well, you obviously got it. You must have wanted to see me or you wouldn't have taken time off and sailed here single-handed from Lefkas.

"My mum Jennifer and Bridges my dad made a big mistake. They had something they both knew was special, but only let it last a week instead of a lifetime. I'm not going to make that same mistake. We had a week together last year. I want more, Dan. A lot more. I want a lifetime with you. My mum's life was dull, mine has been dull up to now, but my dad was a rock star! I won't waste my life by living without someone I love. It's in my genes not to be dull! My mum was a rock chick. I need to find my own bit of rock and roll, and I want you to be my star, my front man. If, of course, you can cope with a damaged, slightly unsure woman like me.

"Yes, it was love at first sight, but I want to believe in that. I need to. You know what I like about you, Dan? You've got spirit but absolutely no need to control or dominate me or any relationship we might have. We'll always be equals. We'll respect and care for each other. I know we only had a week together, but we snatched moments which were more exciting and more enjoyable than whole months I've spent with other men I've been with. Making love with you was the best… it was really the best. I told my dad about you, and he said that if you had made such an impression on me, I should chase you. Tell you. Love you with all the passion in my heart.

"Dan, can I charter you and the yacht, so you can take me away and show me these islands? I won't make you promise that we'll be together forever. I can only tell you that I know that I'm in love with you. When I saw you tie up your boat an hour ago, I just knew we should be together.

Look, I'm going to get the bill and then I'm checking out of the hotel. I want you to take me somewhere we can be alone. That's if you want to, of course? I'm damaged, second-hand and a bit… no, I'm very needy. But I'm in love with you, Dan. Show me how to live, show me how to let go and how to love. Let's set a new course and let's have a brilliant life together. I really owe it to my mum as well. Oh, and my dad. He is a famous rock guitarist after all!"

The waiter watched as the young man leaped up and threw his arms around the woman at the taverna table, the best one at the front.

The young skipper picked her up and held her tight, lifting her until her feet left the ground. He swung her round and kissed her lips; kissed the exposed tattoo on her shoulder and arm. She kissed him back. Then together, hand in hand, they walked towards the hotel making plans. As they left the taverna the waiter scrolled through the music and selected a song. The sound system thumped out an old track by a band called Broken Bikini. It was the band's second number one single, a song called "Stella, You're a Star".

The woman recognised it and stood still. She clenched her fist and raised it in the air, and then she shouted:

"Hey, world, my DAD wrote this!" Then, in a faltering voice and with tears running down her cheeks, she shouted out:

"Hey, this one's for you, Mum! He wrote it for you. He loved you. He really, really did. You lost your dream man, Mum, but I've found mine, and I'm never, ever letting him go."

Falling Stars

Hi, Emma,

I'm writing this email from a taverna on the island here in Greece. Do you remember, I told you I was coming? Mum's got Jack so it's a nice break, although I really haven't had a chance to enjoy this idyllic little island yet, there's so much going on in my head, but that's about to change! Sorry I haven't been in touch, I've been so wrapped up in all this. I didn't tell you exactly what I was doing as we've been trying to keep it quiet but I'm back with the old cast members from the show, to see if we can sort things out.

The TV company and the channel which broadcast the programme want us to make a reunion special, a sort of "What happened next to the flatmates?"

There's no doubt that *Sharing the Sink* was one of the most successful TV romantic situation comedies of its time. It had elements of all those American programmes about young people living together in a big city, but it had so much more as well. I remember seeing the script for the first episode – you know, the one where my character Jessica meets Twigs and Tara while answering an advert for a flat share? Then Daniel turns up along with Adam, he was the one who didn't get into the flat. Well, it just happened! Brilliant writing of course. Remember those first few scenes where the characters gave each other "tests" to see which of us... or rather which of them... could best live together in the flat? Hilarious, especially that dialogue with the balloons and the corset; that's still voted one of the funniest scenes ever on TV. Well, the two people who wrote it had both had successes with other shows, and when they got together to create this it was bound to succeed, and of course it did. Well, until that one night of madness and sex ruined it.

I still remember the auditions. I didn't think I had a chance, there were some known faces there as well, and I was amazed when I was picked, straight after finishing my theatre and arts course. They said they were looking for young unknowns, partly because they wanted it to be new and raw, but also because we were cheap! They were offering the lowest rates they could, but it was such a great opportunity. Interestingly they're now offering us USA rates for a two-part special, which my agent says will lead to another series or a spin off or two involving the four of us.

I'm told the even though they're yet to be made, the reunion specials have already got interest in advance from America, Canada, Australia, New Zealand and half of Europe, including all of Scandinavia! Do you realise how many fan letters we still get? After all this time! The DVDs sell well, and those conventions!

Well, I thought they were joking when we were all invited to a TV soaps and sit coms fans weekend event. Two of us took part – not me, I wasn't going to be in the same room as Josh or Rivers. Josh was Twigs and Rivers played Daniel, of course. I wasn't keen on seeing Kate either; she was Tara in the show, remember?

Fact is, though, the money has all but run out, only one of us has had any acting work since that show ended… or rather since the show failed because we took it off the air with that blazing row. So we've got together this week to try to overcome our issues, sign the contracts and go for the specials. My agent says if the others signed and I didn't, then the TV company might just cast someone else to play Jessica, my character. I guess it largely comes down to me. I feel I owe it to my son Jack to provide him with a decent standard of living; we've been struggling recently. All I have is the acting classes I get from the stage school in town, and the annual Christmas Panto work I get at the local theatre, but I can only play on "I was once on TV, I was Jessica in *Sharing the Sink*" for so long. It'll stop soon and they'll get some other dusty celeb for Cinderella or Dick Whittington. Hopefully though that may not bother me soon.

It was weird seeing the other three again. It was quite painful actually, really pretty bad. I was sick twice on the plane from worrying about it. We all made our way here to the island separately. I found myself on the same ferry as Kate but I didn't even say hello. Instead I shrank back in my seat, turned up the MP3 player, stared at the eBook reader and hid behind my sunglasses. She looks great. Mind you, she always did. She was glamour and I was the academic. I played Jessica, a young doctor at a local hospital. Tara's character was a model. Daniel was a lawyer and Twigs was the singer in a band if you remember. So Kate, AKA Tara of course, made money after the show ended by getting a part in that daytime soap. She played a teacher who had an affair with someone. Rather apt I thought… meow! I can't remember really as I hardly ever watched it.

She was always very pretty though. Then after the soap part ended she did that photo shoot for that lads' magazine. It looked good but was a bit distasteful I thought. The magazine played on her former role as Tara in our show. They put a banner on the front page reading "Tara's tits uncovered at last!" The shot was a picture of her smiling and with her index fingers just covering her nipples. She was obviously proud of it; I thought it was a bit poor. You know, they approached me through my agent too! Would I do a double photo shoot with her? They were going to headline it: "TV's Jessica and Tara – Sharing the Sink and Sharing the Shot, Both Naked and Both Very Hot!" Despite being offered £5,000 I said "No, thanks". Much as I needed the money I didn't want my son having that passed around his school friends in years to come. Besides I'd recently had a baby then and I wasn't going to stand up and be compared with her. She's a bloody model after all!

So Josh got a few voiceovers for adverts. He appeared in one of them as well, it was a TV commercial for sofas. He did get a couple of small parts in that police series, *On The Beat*, and a few parts in a couple of plays on Radio Four. I guess we were so associated with *Sharing the Sink* that people didn't want us; also of course because everyone in the industry knew we'd refused to work together and we'd taken the show off the air. That doesn't help.

Rivers hit the bottle. He couldn't face it, not being able to get in free to all those clubs and celebrity events he used to love. He was done for drinking and driving and lost his licence. He hit the bottle and was photographed going into a rehab clinic. It was all over the papers: "*Sharing the Sink* Star Goes Down the Drain!" And worse.

He got quite low, I think. Mind you, the bastard deserved it after what he did to me. I didn't tell you, did I? Well, it's time I did.

We'd recorded, and they'd edited and transmitted, the first series of *Sharing the Sink*, which had gone down an absolute storm. *It's what TV has been waiting for,* said one of the reviewers. We were on everyone's lips, we were photographed, our back stories told, we were the highest-rating romantic comedy on TV in the UK. We won "Best New Show" and "Best Newcomers", and Josh won "Best Actor" in the TV awards, much to Rivers annoyance, of course. He always thought he was best… best at everything. So a second series was commissioned and our wages shot up, not quite to US levels but triple the first series money, with a promise of another doubling of the pay for series three which would inevitably follow. Problem is, of course, it didn't.

As the second series started I realised I really liked Josh. I felt I couldn't ask him out as I knew we had to keep our relationship professional. I did think about him a lot though; he's a great actor and a lovely person. Then it got complicated. I decided I would ask him out, just for a meal after work, and he said yes. We went from the studio into central London and spent an evening at a pasta restaurant in Holborn. We both wore dark glasses and I had a beanie hat pulled down over my head as we didn't want any gossip. We walked back towards the tube station hand in hand, but then we went our separate ways. We agreed that we'd have to put anything between us on hold until after we'd finished the series, to keep it all professional.

I had made a mental note that after we finished recording the last show in this series I would take Josh out, and then, hopefully, home to bed. However, we did end up in bed a few weeks later, but not as I'd have wanted it. Halfway through the second series Kate starting getting shirty. She complained that Tara, her character, wasn't wearing nice enough clothes. Tara was a model, after all, and would be wearing more expensive, sexier outfits, Kate said. It was a pre-watershed show so she couldn't go too mad, but she wanted more cleavage revealed almost every week. I'm sure she'd have done it topless if she could have! She had a real go, and then Rivers dived in and complained that his character, Daniel, was underdressed too. The poor costume woman had a breakdown, literally, and left the show.

Increasingly Rivers and Kate wanted more and more of the action and better lines. If I had a top line she'd steal it and jump in with it whatever the script said. The director was not impressed, but in the end the show was becoming more Rivers and Kate, especially after the on-screen "kiss and cuddle" they had at the end of the second episode of series two. That was supposed to be funny, it was a romantic comedy after all, but it wasn't what they were expecting. Rivers's character Daniel, the great "I am an amazing stud", turned out to be a virgin and had to text Twigs, who was Josh's character, from the bedroom to ask for tips on bedding Tara. Rivers thought his character being a virgin reflected on him as an actor and his own reputation! What an ego… unbelievable. Still he wasn't happy and became more and more agitated as the filming went on.

Josh suggested the four of us needed to "bond a bit more" and maybe we should spend a weekend together, to help each other learn lines and feel more comfortable in our characters. We all agreed and hired a cottage in

Essex. It was beautiful, all old beams and big fireplaces. So on the Friday night we stocked up with booze and food and drove up the A12 to the cottage near Witham. Unbeknown to us, Rivers had brought some drugs.

Friday night was gentle and nice and we all seemed to be getting on really well. There were four small bedrooms and mine had a great view across the fields behind the house. Saturday morning we had a walk and found a quiet country pub for lunch, a ploughman's and a half of the local beer, all very pleasant. Then we went back to the cottage and spent the afternoon reading our lines together.

Evening came, and Josh lit a fire in the big inglenook fireplace in the sitting room. It was lovely. He and I spent the next hour in the kitchen cooking the "almost" ready meal we'd brought with us. It was great to be with him, and I kind of let myself dream that we'd make a couple one day. So we ate and drank, and drank some more, and then ate some chocolates.

I found myself drifting away. I couldn't always focus and the music was sort of waving in and out. I realised we'd somehow taken something. So did Josh. He asked outright if anyone had spiked the food or drink. Rivers laughed and said we needed to chill, and he'd ensured we would. He admitted he'd given us all a "little something" and suggested we should dance. Kate laughed and got up to join him. I just sat there, feeling worried and unsure. Josh looked at me and I could see he was finding it difficult to focus as well. Soon Kate and Rivers were stripping off their clothes and dancing naked. They called to me to do the same but I said I didn't want to, although I was giggling. It was impossible for me to stop, thanks to whatever it was Rivers had given us.

The next thing I knew Kate and Rivers were undressing me, pulling my clothes off. All I could do was laugh even though I really wasn't finding it funny, and when I tried to stop them, they tickled me until I was helpless and agreed they could strip me if they stopped the tickling. I was really scared I was going to wee myself. Josh suggested they should leave me alone but he was shouted down. Soon I was naked and started dancing too. I felt maybe I should join in. What the hell? I started finding it funny, and after a while Josh joined us, taking his clothes off too.

I lost track of time and events but I do know I found myself in bed with Josh and it was fabulous. I remember a tiny voice of reality and sanity in my drug-addled brain telling me I was OK and this was fine. Expect it wasn't. I fell asleep but woke up alone and on my side with my knees up.

Josh wasn't there, but someone else was. It was Rivers; he climbed in next to me, and pushed himself into me. He didn't ask, talk or anything, he just entered me, holding my knees so I couldn't straighten my legs. I couldn't stop him. Then he grabbed my breasts and squeezed them really hard. The next thing I realised was that Kate was in bed with us too. She took Rivers's place and started kissing me. Her hands were on my breasts and then between my legs. I tried to push her away, I didn't want this, but Rivers was holding my arms and she was laughing and moaning. She grabbed my hand and held it between her legs.

When it was over I literally crawled to the bathroom. I turned on the shower and sat under it for what seemed like hours. I was crying because I'd broken my agreement with Josh, and then I'd been raped and assaulted by two people I thought I could trust. I crawled, wet, naked and cold, along the corridor to the fourth bedroom where Josh was. He was asleep but I climbed in next to him. I felt safer with him than on my own in case Rivers wanted some more.

Sunday was quiet, but we all had headaches and hangovers and agreed not to discuss the night before, although Josh and I both told Rivers he had no right to give us drugs like that. He'd actually raped me, I suppose Kate had too, but what could I do? Really, what was the evidence? Would the others back me up? Josh might but he wasn't in the room when it happened, he was out cold. Kate would have sided with Rivers and said I consented, I was sure of that.

We headed back to London in the car we'd hired for the weekend, and went back to our separate homes. I did send Josh a card saying I hadn't intended it to happen like that but I would love to have a relationship with him after we'd finished the filming in a few weeks' time. He sent me a text saying, *Just say when, Sarah, just say when. I feel the same xx*

This was mid-way through the second series. When we went into the studio to prepare to record another episode on the Monday morning, the crew had no idea that the actors had spent the weekend learning their lines, in bed with each other. By then I knew I could never work with Rivers or Kate again, but I had to finish the series. It later emerged why Kate's character Tara was getting more lines and better scenes as well; turns out she was sleeping with the Executive Producer.

Kate has always threatened to reveal what happened that weekend in an article for a sleazy Sunday paper, telling the world all the "Secrets from

Sharing the Sink". So far she's resisted because Rivers has got some pretty damning stuff against her. He found out that before she did our TV show she once auditioned for porn work in Holland. She did an audition tape with a so-called porn "agent", except he wasn't, he just filmed her stripping and fiddling with herself and then doing it with him, the "agent". He sold it to a pay-to-view website. She was wearing a wig but Rivers knew it was her because of the tattoo on her buttock. What he was doing searching pay-to-view porn sites is another matter; however, he downloaded it and threatened to upload it on to more general sites if she said anything to embarrass him.

None of us actually had girl or boyfriends during the filming of that series. Well, apart from Rivers, but he never stayed faithful to anyone, and he told us it "didn't matter", she would "expect him" to play the field. So afterwards Rivers took liberties every time we were in the dressing rooms unless I locked the door. He'd grope me and Kate. She didn't mind that much it seemed, she laughed it off and was clearly having casual sex with him. Josh backed off completely and went very quiet. He wouldn't discuss it, he just smiled, quite warmly usually. I felt really uncomfortable about the whole thing, I remember someone saying work affairs are OK but often end dangerously, "never poo on your own doorstep" or something like that, so I knew however difficult it was, I had just to stay friends with Josh until after the series had ended.

We carried on, but tensions mounted. There were the arguments about who had the best lines, the best shots, and the best clothes. Kate's and Rivers's characters became the dominant leads on screen, and always took the front spots in interviews and publicity shots. Then a few weeks later I realised that I hadn't started my period. I was two weeks late. I did a test in the ladies' loo by the dressing rooms and felt sick when I saw the result. I was pregnant. It could only have been Rivers's or Josh's baby. Then I really felt sick. I went back to make-up and asked Alice the make-up supremo to re-do my face. The tears had left their mark and it was obvious that I'd been crying.

I've never told you about my son Jack's father, have I? Remember I always said it was just an old boyfriend who was no longer around. Well, that's the truth. So I went on set and somehow staggered my way through my lines. Luckily I didn't have many scenes that week, but the ones I did have were hard to play. I felt so self-conscious when the camera moved towards me, and I knew the director was zooming in for a close up when Twigs, that's Josh of course, delivered some killer line about my red sweater staining his white tee shirt after a laundry mix up. There was then an old-fashioned joke fest about mixing up clothes and who might be wearing whose knickers and so on.

I forced smiles on cue as the script demanded and hoped the director wouldn't want too many retakes. Josh could tell there was something wrong and asked if I was OK while they were resetting the cameras and lighting rig for the next scene. I smiled and remember saying something like: "Oh, just a bit under par, thanks."

I somehow carried on, with my head and heart in turmoil. When that day's filming finally finished, I went home, and cried.

There was one more show to film the following week. I locked myself away that weekend, concentrating on my script and wondering who the father was. Rivers was the Alpha male so I guess it was his sperm that had got through. In fact I couldn't remember how things between Josh and me actually ended that night, whether or not he'd come inside me or not, but it was clear that Rivers had. So I'd had unprotected sex with *two* men in one night. Why hadn't either of them used condoms?

At that point in our careers we should have been on the crest of a wave of enthusiasm, we were the darlings of British TV and we were in this unreal, tinsel town, luvvieland. We were supposed to be on "cloud nine" but instead it had become a cloud burst, washing away our dreams.

As we went into the studio for the recording of the last show in the second series, I asked both Rivers and Josh to meet me in my dressing room. They turned up just after the first read through of the script, during a coffee break. Josh smiled and asked if I was OK. Rivers followed him in and shouted at me. He said I wasn't pulling my weight and our scenes were making him look dull. I started crying. Then the director, Paul, walked in. He said he wanted a decent show for the end of the series. They'd brought in some big guest-star comedian to play the part of a plumber mending a bunged up toilet in the flat, and there was an inquest into who had blocked it. I wasn't finding the script at all funny, I thought it was too crude and started to query the lines I was supposed to be delivering. Kate then stormed in, throwing her script down and shouting about how annoyed she was having to wear the same outfit in this episode as she did in one two weeks before. She said they'd have to change it as she wasn't going on set without something better. The director then announced he'd be leaving at the end of the show and wouldn't be involved in series three. He said he couldn't carry on with the Executive Producer telling him what shots to take, and besides he'd found out why the exec was always telling him to favour Kate. It was because they were sleeping together!

She laughed and said it was because she deserved the best shots and the best scenes because she was the real talent in the cast. Rivers grabbed her shoulders and shouted at her. I'll always remember what he said: "You pathetic little shit, you're not a good actress, you're just good at screwing the right people. I'll bet you were screwing him before the audition. Was he a porn 'agent' too, like the bloke in Amsterdam?"

Kate squealed and gasped: "You can never be certain that's me, Rivers. I'll sue if you keep on saying that!" He interrupted her, sneering: "No one else has a tattoo like that on their buttocks. It's you, Kate. It's you, sitting there on a black leather sofa, opening your legs and..." But before he could give any more lurid details she shut him up by thumping in the mouth. He fell back with blood dribbling from his lip.

He mumbled with his hand over his mouth, blood seeping through his fingers: "You've broken my tooth, you bitch!" Josh said we should all calm down. Kate then hit poor Josh too, who was only trying to help, and then she ran out and left the studio. Rivers went home. Josh and I sat with Paul for a few minutes and tried to work out what we could do. Then I started crying and said:"I'm pregnant."

The day dissolved into chaos. The head of the production company came round to see us individually at our homes. Although remaining sympathetic and supportive, he made it quite clear that we had a contractual obligation to finish the shoot and record the last programme. He said he'd get the writers to include a few "flashbacks" from earlier episodes, and have the characters reflect on some of the funnier incidents that had happened over the past series. That meant we could cut down on the number of new scenes we'd need to film. He also said he'd try to reduce the number of scenes with all four of us together so we could avoid contact with each other as much as possible. They even assigned each of us a "runner", who would escort us round the building, fetch coffee etc. so that we would have minimal contact with each other. Another director had also been brought in to direct the last episode.

You'd be surprised, Emma, how often this sort of thing happens. It's an intense working relationship and emotionally draining so it's not surprising that blow ups like this happen on set. Mind you, it doesn't help when two of the cast has raped another, one of them probably impregnating her as well.

We somehow got through it, although Kate was just horrible to everyone, like a teenager in a temper tantrum. Rivers was awful too. He sidled up to me just before we filmed a scene with the four of us in it and whispered: "If you ever suggest I might be the father of your bastard child, I'll tell the world what a whore you are."

He added menacingly that he had taken pictures of me and Kate during our ten-minute fumble when she'd groped me, and that he'd publish them online if he had to. He also said if I ever made a claim against him for paternity he'd demand access to the child, and would "poison the kid" against me. What a bastard! He said that he and Josh looked similar so either of them could be the father.

I cried as the recording started. They had to write in a line about my character having accidentally rubbed chilli powder into her eye. I could certainly act that OK, they were real tears. Once we'd finished the shoot, the post-series party was cancelled. Caterers had brought in nibbles, a cake and champagne to celebrate the end of another great series. We all just walked out, leaving our costumes on the floor of our dressing rooms. We didn't even say goodbye to each other or to the crew, and that was sad as the crew had been great, and no one had said a word to the press about the frictions between us.

So I went home. The third series was cancelled. Reporters asked why. We each put out a statement, saying we'd had professional differences, and left it like that. There were rumours and reports that there had been an affair or two, but nothing was proved and we all kept quiet.

I moved away from London to somewhere cheaper. My agent tried to get me more work, but it was difficult as I said earlier. He was also the others' agent too, and because of the rumours and the fact that we'd taken a show off the air, no one was that keen to give us a contract for more TV or film work. Apart from Kate who "somehow" got a part in that daytime soap.

When Jack was born I didn't tell anyone who the father might be. My mother and father asked but I refused to say. Luckily I had the money from the first two series, which allowed me to buy a small house and gave me a few quid in the bank to live on. I got the job teaching at the weekend drama school, and some work in local schools, helping with end-of-year plays and so on. Then there were the Christmas pantomimes. At first I was still "currency" so I got a decent rate, playing a lead in reasonable-sized venues. Then it tailed off and I ended up doing regular appearances in a local panto. It paid, but not very much, although it was just about enough to cover the bills and keep me and Jack fed.

I had a boyfriend or two, as you know, but nothing worked out. The only person I'd ever really liked was Josh. He was always kind, and that weekend before we'd had the drunken orgy... god, what a word... he'd been tender and loving. But how could I ever contact him again and ask him out with me when I probably had Rivers's child? Apparently a year or so ago Rivers and Josh met in a pub in London and a fight broke out. Our agent told me about it, said they were fighting over me and what Rivers did that weekend.

So that brings us to this week on the island and the reunion. Now you can see why I was dreading it. When I arrived at the villa which the agent had hired for us, he met me at the door. Before leading me in, he explained I was the last to arrive and we were all to be "calm and adult" about whatever had happened in the past. My heart was in my mouth.

I walked in to the big living room-cum-kitchen of the villa, its white walls setting off the pine furniture with thick cord cushions. Kate and Rivers sat together. Rivers was looking like a peacock, with his fake tan, dyed hair, expensive holiday shirt and white linen trousers. He half smiled and nodded at me. Kate got up and gave me a kiss on both cheeks before saying how lovely it was to see me again.

Josh got up, looking worried. He hugged me fiercely, whispering in my ear: "Sarah, I was hoping you'd call, you know. I still have the card you sent me after that horrible weekend." I smiled and said nothing.

Then the agent said the money on offer from the TV company was big, the potential was enormous, and the rewards from another full series could be fantastic. He pointed out that the show was still being repeated ten years on and people really wanted more. They wanted to know what had happened to our characters. He said it didn't matter what had happened between us in our private lives, we had a duty to ourselves and to our fans to, in his words: "Get your acts together and bloody well act."

We listened to what the TV company was proposing regarding the storyboard for the two "Whatever happened to" episodes, and what each character's storyline would be. Turns out they'd got my character and Josh's living together in the flat, with the other two both having recently split up from their girl or boyfriend and having to move back in "just for a while". It was plausible. I found myself sitting next to Josh and our legs touched.

By the evening it all looked very promising until Rivers said he'd arranged with the little hotel in the port to bring us a takeaway from their kitchen. We had their menu so we could just ring them when we were ready and they'd bring it up to us. Yannis the hotelier was really sweet, typically Greek, hospitable and welcoming. Turns out he owned the villa too or maybe his brother did, something like that.

It was all going well until Rivers said, "OK, I'll ring him, just to make sure he doesn't put anything extra in the drink!"

That was it. Josh leaped up and grabbed him. They wrestled each other to the floor, knocking over a glass and a bottle of red wine, which washed across the stone tiles like blood. Kate pulled Josh off Rivers and I grabbed her. I still hadn't forgiven her for what she did to me that night in the cottage, and I was about to lose my temper big time when the agent screamed at us all to stop.

An hour and a half later the food was there and we'd all had showers, unpacked and calmed down. At the agent's suggestion, Rivers then apologised to all of us for his actions at the cottage, and for the way he'd behaved overall. He begged me to agree to the show going ahead; said I was the one holding them all back. Kate too apologised and started crying. Josh just held me and said he was sorry too; he should have protected me that night and should never have left me alone.

I turned to Rivers and said:

"Your son Jack is nearly ten years old. He's a lovely boy. I thought you ought to know."

Rivers shook his head and said, "Sarah, you're wrong. I am infertile, I always have been. I found out five years ago when I wanted to be a sperm donor. Apparently I have a genetic abnormality. I cannot produce sperm, only seminal fluid. I can never have a child."

He then surprised us all by saying, with tears of real remorse in his eyes:

"By the way, Kate and Sarah, I have destroyed any photographic evidence of that night and I had no right to take it in the first place. I really am sorry for what I did. Truly. Please forgive me."

I turned to Josh, with tears of relief and joy in my eyes, and said: "Then you're my boy's dad! Josh, it could only have been you! You've got a son called Jack!"

We hugged and kissed and then we both cried. He wanted to see pictures of Jack, so after we'd eaten we walked down to this taverna and sat at this very table and I showed him photos of our child, from birth to the most recent ones that I had on my laptop, some taken just last week.

Josh was so sweet. He said: "Sarah, I'm single, I have no girlfriend right now. Can I be a proper dad to Jack? Can I be your husband in real life as well as in the reunion episodes of *Sharing the Sink*?"

We drank, we laughed, we cried. We went back to the villa together and, yes, we shared a room last night, and yes, we made love, beautiful love. Josh and I are going to live together, he's moving in with me and Jack.

This morning we signed the contracts with the others so the reunion episodes can go ahead. We've chartered a yacht to go and see the island from the sea. I want to swim with him in clear blue water, to feel his wet skin against mine, to sunbathe naked with him on the deck of a yacht, and to feel him inside me again.

Before we leave I've come down here to the taverna to email this to you and tell you how happy we both are. He'll be here in a moment as the yacht's booked for ten o'clock and it's five to now. I'll ring when I get back to the UK, and you'd better start thinking about what to wear at our wedding! It'll have to wait until after these two new episodes are recorded, though, as they want to start shooting in a month, to hit the tenth anniversary of the show ending. So it looks like Josh and I will be *Sharing the Sink* at home and at work, and sharing the bed as well!

Hey, I'm going now. Here he comes, my future husband! Emma, it's so nice to be in love.

Hugs,
Sarah
Xx

The waiter watched as a man he vaguely recognised walked up to the table by the water. The pretty woman sitting there closed her laptop and smiled up at him. He saw the man kiss her then lead her to the gangplank of a waiting yacht. Once they were aboard, the boat's skipper untied the mooring lines and motored the yacht out of the bay towards the open sea. The couple kissed as they waved to three other people watching from the quayside.

The waiter smiled. He could see the couple on the yacht were very much in love.

Family Secrets

The waiter at the taverna watched as the young woman at the table near the water picked out an envelope from her bag. She kissed it and put it back, and then, after opening her laptop and connecting to the taverna's wi-fi, she began to compose an email.

Hi, I know it's been a while, but I've just got to tell you something that's almost believable! It still seems unreal. I'm sitting at a taverna on the island. You know, the one I told you I was coming to, to scatter Mum's and Dad's ashes like they asked me to? I was going to ring but it's just too amazing to tell you on the phone. I have to tell you in this email.

You remember my dad had made me promise that when he died, I was to take his and Mum's ashes – which he kept in that awful plastic urn in the conservatory (why?!!) – and scatter them in one of the places they used to walk or sit on this island, where they always had their holidays? Well, after Dad died… and thanks again for coming to the funeral last month. There were so few people there, I thought it was sad; they died quite young as well. I can't believe they barely made their fifties… anyway I finally got round to It. I flew out on Sunday, but it's turned out very differently from how I thought it would. Honestly it's just incredible. You'll be surprised, I'm sure!

I've got this week off school as it's half-term, so I went back to the house – their house, my old home – to collect the ashes. It's still for sale, by the way. The estate agent says there's lots of interest, but no offers yet. Luckily they're handling all the viewings and enquiries. I don't want to go there any more than I have to. It reminds me of a dull boring childhood with loving but uninspiring, grey parents.

Anyway, I went in, and moved the piles of junk mail and other crap. Amazing, isn't it? Even when you tell people your parents are dead they still send them letters including offers of life insurance. Er, a bit late! So I checked the house. Empty rooms. Cooker, fridge and freezer unplugged and with gaping doors. I half expected to find them asleep in the bedroom. I remember walking in there during cold, frightening, childhood nights to see them sleeping together, quietly drifting towards dawn.

I picked up Dad's ashes, which were sealed in a brown, round barrel-like container from the undertaker's, and I lifted Mum's urn from the conservatory floor. It was dusty, but warmed by the early-morning sun. It was odd because I paused at the front door when I took their ashes out, a sort of last goodbye even though they'd already left. As soon as the house is sold I'm going to get a house clearance mob in to empty it. I've got my own stuff and don't want to go back there again.

The drive to the airport was OK and the flight was good. In three hours I was landing in Corfu. I love the architecture there. The old Venetian waterfront is lovely and the streets in the main town are brilliant. Lots of great shops too! It's also sunny and hot, which compared to home is wonderful. I was worried I'd be stopped if they found the ashes in my suitcase, but no one did. So I walked out of the airport building into the sunlight and got into a taxi, which took me to the port where I took the Flying Dolphin as the hydrofoils are called. It was a bit like a bus on runners, skimming over the water! Great fun if a little bumpy at times!

The island is gorgeous and I can see why Mum and Dad used to like coming here so much. I went to the hotel where they'd stayed. It was the same one they came to, year in, year out, they loved it. It's really small, just six rooms, and the hotelier, Yannis, remembered them straight away. He'd been expecting me. Said he knew I'd be coming. Anyway the room is great, with fantastic views of the boats in the bay. It's just beautiful.

It was sad thinking they'd never see or enjoy this again when they loved it so much. They used to come here three or even four times a year. Dad hadn't been here since he went sick, of course, although he always thought he'd recover right to the end. Sadly, as you know, that end took two years in coming. He never expected Mum to die so soon either, just two months after her diagnosis. It's been a rough few years.

Walking around the small town with its narrow alleys was lovely. It was good to follow in their footsteps, seeing the restaurants and tavernas they told me they use to eat in and where they'd had so many happy times. Everyone here is so friendly too. I hired a car and drove around the island exploring the tiny hamlets. It's not that big and the west coast has some stunning cliffs. Not much in the way of beaches, they're mainly small and covered with shingle but quite delightful even so, and happily no rows of industrial sunbeds and tanning by numbers! Everywhere I went I took their ashes, those two little containers holding all that remained of my parents. It was a very odd feeling. Dad had never said exactly where to put them, so I wanted to explore and reach a decision. Then I got the text.

I told you I was worried it would all end in tears, didn't I? Peter and me.

Well, it's over. Not great timing, of course, as I could have done with some bedroom distraction and a nice illicit evening out when I get home. However, it isn't to be. As you know, and you did warn me against it, it was bonkers for me to start an affair with a married man ten years older than I am. You were right, Sal, he was simply looking for a fling and fancied a younger model. And I really believed at first that no one would get hurt. Why? I thought his marriage must be buggered anyway or he wouldn't be playing away. But nope, he wanted it all, me and his wife. I don't regret it because it was fun at the time and he was very keen to please, if you know what I mean! Unlike others I've had the misfortune to find myself in bed with.

Well, his wife found out, of course. She read a message from me on his phone and confronted him. He immediately told her he would stop seeing me and dumped me by text on Monday, saying he couldn't get through on the phone. Liar! You know, I don't mind if he dumps me… well, I do… but I understood it was never going to be a long-term love affair. It was always just an exciting interlude, a fling. He told me he had an "open marriage" and his wife "didn't mind". Well, clearly she did!

God, why do I do this? They're all disasters, my relationships, aren't they? What do I do wrong? The two before him were awful too. I met them both on dating sites. The first one… yes, Richard, you met him, the architect… well, he looked OK, sounded nice, had a decent job, but was just soooo dull! In fact, he reminded me of my parents! Playing computer games revolving around demons and wizards and trolls and stuff isn't really my idea of a good time, especially when he invited me to a weekend fantasy war games convention! I should have guessed when I found out he still lived with his mother.

Then there was Paul, who was great on the surface. We went out for a few weeks, do you remember him? We did that double date with you and Dave at that pizza place. He was a teacher and we had a lot in common, or so I thought, until I discovered he was in that weird men-only club. Wives and partners were invited to a club dinner once a year, but had to dress in a certain way and call people by strange names! What century does he think we live in? More to the point, who did he think he was going out with? Sorry, but if he's in a club that treats women as second-class citizens then I'm not in his club, ever. You remember I told you what happened? How I came round to see you afterwards and threw my bag across your sitting room in disgust. Mind you, you would have been proud of me for sticking up for myself. Halfway through the starter, when I realised what the club was like, I stood up and told him in a very loud voice that I wasn't participating in some outdated, antiquated event, I was leaving. I said his calls would no longer be answered and his emails would hit the junk folder. Hah!

Some irritating little idiot in a dinner jacket said: "Madam, we wait until we are invited to leave the table." I just turned round and said: "Grow up, you pathetic twat." That caused a few sharp intakes of breath! I pushed past him. Honestly, if he'd dared to say anything else I'd have kneed him in the balls. Always assuming he had any, of course! So, needless to say, Paul didn't call again. One day I'll find someone more suitable, I guess.

Anyway back to the ashes. I made my mind up when I found the lighthouse on top of the cliff on the northernmost tip of the island. It's not especially tall but makes quite a statement. From there you can see Corfu and the mainland as well. Below, waves crash against the rocks, and then to the south-east is the sweep of the bay, which is stunning, with the bluest water you can imagine.

So yesterday I walked up there with both the little containers, and at exactly midday I undid them and let the ashes float free. Luckily the wind was light. The grey flakes of what remained of my parents fell gently down the cliff face and over the scrub and the sea below. There they were, united in death, dust on the wind all that was left of them apart from memories. Two lives that had been lived in such a dull pedestrian way… their main aim, it always seemed, was to get through life and die without being seriously embarrassed, or doing anything that was in any way exciting, adventurous or interesting. Or so I thought!

As I watched the ashes disappear I didn't cry. I'd done all that when they'd both died. I was just relieved that I'd carried out their last wishes. I stood there for a while in the bright sunshine and rising heat, by the white wall of the lighthouse compound. I was in a bit of a daze until a couple came walking by and said hello. I drank some water as I watched a spider pounce on a big black bug caught in its web. Then I headed back down the narrow track to the port below. To cheer myself up I went shopping. There aren't many places to spend money in this delightful little town, but I found a lovely "hippy" shop with the most fantastic tops. I bought one; in fact I got two, one for you as well! You'll love it; it's just your colour.

They had some really nice little wristbands and anklets, all in hessian and natural cottons. I bought a selection of those as well; they'll make great Christmas presents.

Then I came to this taverna on the front; it's my favourite, just lovely. There are really comfy seats, some with big, dreamy cushions, and a fantastic view across the water. I could spend a week just sitting here. The music's good too. The people you see are amazing. I'm sure I saw that actress who's in that crime series, you know, the one about the inspector in the Northern town? God, my memory! And I saw some guy I'm sure is a big old rock star. He was holding hands with a woman and drinking cocktails.

There are some people about with great taste in clothes and others with, well, let's say none at all. It's just embarrassing! There's a woman at a table not far from me right now wearing a dreadful yellow see-through top with a blue bra underneath! It just doesn't work. Take it off, girl! Wear the top on its own. It'll look better. Then, to make it even worse, she's wearing green shorts! Why? I'm half expecting to see a seersucker boob tube and a white ra-ra skirt next. Oh, well, I guess I'm not exactly the epitome of haute couture myself, in my denim skirt and tee shirt.

So after scattering the ashes and cheering myself up with the shopping and coffee… oh, and a cake, a lovely cake, a moist orange sponge-type cake… I went back to the small hotel, and Yannis the owner asked if I'd "done the ashes". I smiled and said that I had, and asked how he knew. He told me my father had spoken to him shortly before his death. Said Dad had asked him to give me a package when I came to the island. I was a bit puzzled, and looked at him quizzically. He told me the package was in the hotel safe.

Yannis bent down to retrieve a long silver key. He put this into the old lock and turned it. It made a loud "clunk" and then swung open. Yannis picked up a large padded envelope and handed it to me. He told me my parents had kept this package in the hotel and always got it out of the safe on their visits, replacing it when they left. He said my dad had been most insistent that I was the only person who should have it. Yannis said my dad had asked him to tell me to try not to judge them, but to be happy for them.

Feeling really puzzled, I took the package and put it into my bag. I thanked Yannis and walked through the hotel's white-painted lobby out into the sunshine. I went down the little road and crossed the street to this taverna where I'm writing you this email now. Once the waiter had brought my drink I took the envelope out of my bag. I'd had the will, the old family papers and photo albums dating back to before my birth, so what was this? I would soon find out, and would realise then that Pandora's Box had nothing on this! Nothing at all.

Now you've known me since junior school. We shared the important crossroads of life. The first kiss, first love, first betrayal, first dreams and first sex. You know how bloody desperately dull my parents were! Dad with his tediously boring job at the bank, and Mum working as a PA to those solicitors in town. Grey jumpers for him, dark woolen skirts for her. Life for me was so boring. I was always jealous of your home life. Your mum and dad were fun, they did things together, they had a life. Mine were just the pits, so old-fashioned. The house was decorated in beige, everything functional and cheap.

I used to dread friends coming home with me. Every Saturday night was spent sitting in front of the telly. Mum and Dad only seemed to come alive in the build up to their holidays, to the same hotel on the same Greek island, four times a year. They started, I guess, when I was about fourteen. Before that we used to go away and stay in caravans on sites in Cornwall. Then we had a package holiday with another family, a cousin of Mum's, in Spain, and after that every year we'd just have a week as a family in Majorca or France, and then Mum and Dad would go to Greece on their own. I'd stay with friends, usually you, which I preferred as we had a great time.

So over the years they had a lot of these holidays. Inside the package was an envelope with little paper wallets of photographs inside. I opened them, and then I shook, panicked, and quickly put them back. I could hardly believe what I had seen. I thought I'd got the wrong envelope; these were someone else's pictures, not my parents'. Surely not my parents'?!

I hurried away from the taverna table, leaving my half-finished drink and a five-Euro note for the waiter. I rushed back to the hotel, where Yannis the owner smiled and nodded as I barged in and hurried past him, heading for the tiled staircase. I rushed along the corridor to my room, the third on the left at the end. I went in, locked the door and sat down on the bed. I felt shocked, stunned and in denial of what I thought I'd seen. I opened the photograph wallets again.

There was mum, Mary, my very dull, boring mum, except she was wearing a basque and suspenders! They were in a hotel room; it looked suspiciously like the one I was in. There were other people there with them too. Another woman dressed in lingerie; her hair piled high, lipstick thick and full, and heavy, pendulous breasts trying to escape. In the photographs that followed there was my dad, and another man. I recognised him, and went hideously cold. I also realised who the other woman was as well, hidden under all that make up, draped in soft sensual fabrics. The man was one of the partners from the dull, boring solicitor's firm my mum worked for, and the woman was his wife. Stephen and Joan, I think they were called.

So my parents were swingers! You see, the rest of the photographs were just shocking. Most of them were Polaroids, do you remember them? They must have been taken in the seventies. Wow, Mum and Dad looked so much younger. Well, the pictures showed Mum and the other man, Stephen, having sex – making love, shagging – although which it was I'm not sure, but these were very graphic pictures! I was pretty uncomfortable with them, to be honest. You don't think of your mum and dad as lovers, certainly not other people's lovers!

I opened all of the wallets of photographs, and there were scenes with my mum and the other woman… you know, doing it, fingers, mouths, all of it! And there was my dad and the other woman, doing various things. In one photo she was on top of him while her husband was on top of Mum, or Mum was on top of him! I can't describe how I felt, I have nothing to compare it with. I was sad, disgusted, shocked, but yes, even a bit turned on as well, if that doesn't sound sick; and also very happy for them. I just stared, and stared, and I cried as well. I felt somehow betrayed, but also kind of glad, and I said to myself, "Yes, go for it!" I was pleased my parents weren't the dull as ditchwater, boring, staid old relics I'd always thought they were.

There was also a big 10 x 8 picture of the four of them, at the quayside. Clothed, luckily! In fact, dressed very smartly; they were sitting at this very taverna table, the one I'm writing to you from right now, by the water's edge. The waiter must have taken the picture. Dad is holding up a sign written in lipstick on white card, reading "The Holiday Club!" They are all smiling.

Apart from the photographs, in the bottom of the package inside a waterproof bag were three old VHS video tapes. I put the pictures away in the envelope and hid them under the bed. I went downstairs to find Yannis behind the bar; he was chatting and pouring glasses of wine for a couple sitting by the window. I politely waited and then asked him if he knew what was in the package. He just shrugged and smiled and said it was "OK" and my parents and their friends were "very happy together". He gave me a knowing look and smiled again.

It turns out they hired two rooms and who stayed with whom was unpredictable. Sometimes another couple would join them as well, a Dutch couple, a pair of doctors, and yes, they usually used the room I was staying in. That was weird, I can tell you! Yannis told me they used to rent a small motor boat from a man on the quayside and go off together to the beaches on the island nearby. Mum and the other woman were famous for their topless sunbathing by the hotel's small pool, no matter who was about or what time of day it was. They'd walk into the bar topless too at times. Yannis said it was usually OK, then he smiled a little oddly and added: "But not always." He did say though that they were: "like the youngsters, always having fun, and always much in love".

I asked him if he had an old-fashioned VHS player. He said he didn't but he could borrow one from someone in the village. That night he caught me as I walked back from the taverna where I'd eaten and told me he'd set up the VHS in my room. I went in and shut the door behind me. I switched on the light and pulled the curtains, leaving the shutters and windows open to let the cooler night-time breeze take the heat out of the room, which had been shut up for much of the day. Gingerly I retrieved the envelope from beneath my bed and took out the photograph wallets. There at the bottom were the three VHS tapes labelled "holiday memories". I put the first one into the player and pushed the button. It whirred and clunked as the old technology laced up the tape and pushed it against the playing heads.

The small TV set mounted on the wall flickered into action and I found the button to change the source and see the output from the VHS player rather than the TV. More sex, but this time there were others involved too. One showed Mum and three men! Then Mum and two women! I have to say, they were smiling, and Mum was, very embarrassingly, very obviously, enjoying it, as was Dad. Really! God, it's weird and a bit horrid as well. I wish I had a brother or sister to share this with. You're the only person I can tell. It's hardly the sort of thing I can bring up in the staffroom back at school on Monday morning, is it? Not exactly suitable for show and tell!

"Hey, guys, I found out my parents were swingers! Yes, they spent their holidays fucking their brains out with another couple. Anyone want a custard cream?" Not really, I can't, can I? Well, after twenty-four hours of sleepless thought and agonising internal discussion in my head, I realised that Mum and Dad were part of that "free love" generation, they were libertines, hedonists, call it what you will. You know for months after their deaths I felt I never really loved them. Now I realise it's because I never really knew them. I love them now, and I love their memory.

I've decided that I'm actually quite glad that their apparently boring, dull lives were really filled with fun and sexy secrets, and that they didn't just "do it" once a month and on birthdays. I only wish I could tell them that I didn't mind, that I didn't care and that I wasn't judging them or cross. I'm genuinely pleased they had these holidays with their friends. Am I wrong?

I broke the VHS tapes. I decided I didn't want anyone else to see them. Well, who was there to see them? I am an only child and I don't think Mum's sister would be as liberal as me. Mind you, who knows what she's been up to?

I put the broken up tapes into the hotel's big rubbish bin behind the kitchen. Those cassettes have miles of tape in them! I scrunched it up and cut it in several places and made sure it was pushed under a load of vegetable peelings and some old dripping olive oil bottles, so it'll be well and truly unplayable again.

I have kept the photographs, though. Well, just a few of the tamer, milder ones to show you. I will frame the big picture of them posing with their friends outside the hotel. I think it's a lovely photograph, they looked so happy. Thing is, Mum's boss, their "friend", and his wife are still alive. Do I tell them?! I'm not sure, I'm really not sure. Perhaps I should offer them the pictures? Oh, no, I can't. I'll pretend I don't know anything about them. Perhaps I'll just send them a copy of the big shot of the four of them together at the taverna table and say: "Thanks for sharing happy holidays with Mum and Dad. I've been to the island to scatter their ashes, and while I was there I stayed at the hotel and visited the taverna." Then it's up to them to ask questions if they want to, or just ignore it if they prefer.

Yesterday, in the early evening, I had one last walk around the streets of the little port and went back to where I'd scattered their ashes up by the lighthouse on the hill overlooking the sea. I told them I was happy for them and thanked them for letting me in on their little secret. I thanked Yannis at the hotel too. He was so sweet. He said rather cheekily:

"One day you bring your husband here, and maybe some friends too, and have a nice holiday just like your mum and dad did!"

I laughed and told him I didn't yet have a husband, only a string of failed relationships and broken dreams. Oh, well. I'm flying home tomorrow afternoon. I get to Gatwick about three; I'll be home by six so I'll ring you. I'm working Monday, of course, the second half of the term, exams looming. Oh, god, bloody exams.

Please let's get together soon. I really need a drink with a friend so I can talk about all this, and besides I have some interesting, if not disturbing, holiday snaps to show you!!! Hey, at least my mum and dad were ravers, and I thought they were sooo boring... Now I'm sort of proud of them.

You know I've realized this has brought me to a crossroads. I'm no longer going to accept "boring" as the default option for my life. I'm not sure what's going to happen but I'm determined to be more adventurous and find a partner with a bit of spark and ambition, ambition to enjoy life to the full.

Must go, my coffee's cold and I have to pack. Stay well. Talk soon.

Love from a sunny Greek island,

Beccy xxx

The waiter at the taverna watched the young woman close her laptop and put it into her bag. She took out a padded envelope, kissed it and put it back. Then, smiling, she walked towards the hotel.

Making Baby

The waiter at the taverna by the water's edge took a cappuccino to the attractive woman sitting at the table overlooking the sea. As he put down the cup he watched her take her phone from her bag and dial a number. He walked away as her conversation began.

"Hi, Lisa, it's me, Claire. I promised I'd ring. Yes, I'm in Greece, and it's stunning. We're staying on an island in a small resort... well, they all are here! We're in a great hotel. It's really sweet, and Yannis the hotelier is so helpful. I rang because I owe you an explanation as to why I've been quiet recently and it looks like things have come to a head. A lot has happened since we last spoke. Things were looking pretty bloody bleak back then, I can tell you.

"Remember I said we were coming out here to 'solve our problem'? Yes, well, it's a bit more complicated than that. As you know, Sean and I have been together ten years now and I have been desperate to have a baby. I don't care if it's only the one either, I just want *a* baby! But, hey, time really is running out. I'm thirty-nine and statistically the odds of me getting pregnant are getting lower and lower all the time. It's even more important to me now that Mum's ill. She's only likely to survive that hideous disease for another eighteen months to two years. I just want her to see a grandchild. I know it's all she's waiting for, and I'm her only child so it's now or never.

"We have had so many rows over this, Sean and I, been on the verge of splitting up. Really. When we finally found out that he had a low sperm count that was almost it. He got cross, I got cross, and we rowed for days. It was like a shutter coming down. Thanks, you were great at the time, just when I needed a friend the most. I remember I came round to see you at your place and cried. You phoned my boss for me the next morning and said I was sick. You even took the day off work yourself to be with me. It was so good of you, and you know how I was feeling. Really, really down. Thank you for being such a good friend. I know we go back a long way but I appreciate it very much.

"Sorry? ...Why didn't we do the sperm donor bit? IVF and all that? Well, as I think I told you at the time, I don't want any anonymous person to be the biological father of my child. I want to be able to tell him or her, when they are older, that their real dad was... well, whoever and whatever he was.

"So we went into a bit of reclusive hibernation... yes, sorry for the radio silence as it were, but I couldn't really face talking to anyone until we'd got our heads around it. We even went to a marriage guidance counsellor and all of that, but it came down to baby or no baby, and to be honest, it very nearly destroyed us. It really is that important to me. Sean got nasty about it in the end and we were heading for the divorce lawyers.

"So what happened then and are we OK? Well, bear with me, it's a long story. Hope you've got the time! After a few very bleak weeks I read an article in one of the weekend papers about someone using a Nordic sperm donor as they wanted a genetic match. Let's face it, Sean and I are both pretty classic north Europeans so it seemed worth investigating. I really fancied that Scandinavian DNA! There's more of this going on than you might realise. There are quite a few adverts for sperm banks but I wanted actually to meet the donor, to know what he was like.

"So I did some searching and found a few adverts for guys who were fit, intelligent and, yes, Scandinavian. I dug deeper and they had names, real pictures, and seemed to be nice genuine people. I showed Sean and he was a bit perplexed. What was I suggesting? I said it would be a sort of D-I-Y sperm donation. Ideally I'd get it from the donor and... well, you know, the turkey baster thing, those little bulb syringe whatsits, a home insemination kit or whatever it's called! Stick it up, squirt it in and hope the sperm swims to the right place and finds an egg, I guess! All a bit mechanical, but it's just giving nature a hand.

"So I emailed a few of these guys and one really appealed to me. He was a young Danish doctor, living in Copenhagen. He was single and said he'd be happy to offer us a service as it were, but we needed to meet him to collect the sample. It was a condition of his, and that was fine by me as I wanted to meet him too. All we had to do was pay him his air fare, accommodation costs and expenses, and we could meet anywhere in Europe, and more importantly, more or less whenever we wanted to. He did suggest staying in the same place for more than one attempt, as the more donations we had, the better the chance of success.

"After some sleepless nights, many arguments and a few ultimata, largely given by me to Sean, I got back to the Danish guy and we worked out the best time for us re time off work, and my likelihood of conceiving. We also decided to meet him here on this island. The idea was for us then to stay on for a short break and hope that, by sitting relaxing in the sun, it would all start and I'd go home pregnant. Well, it didn't quite work out that way.

"Last weekend we flew to Corfu, got a taxi to the port, and caught the hydrofoil here to the island where we'd arranged to meet Svend. His name actually means 'young man'. Well, that's according to a website I went on to, looking for baby names. I was thinking, you know, maybe I might use it for a middle name if the baby was a boy. So we arrived on Sunday evening and Svend was already here, staying in the same hotel as us as we'd arranged. It's a little place on the hill just on the edge of the resort here. We'd paid for his return flight and his hotel, of course, it's costing us almost a thousand euro all up, but we thought that was cheap for a baby. He said he'd brought a pretty water-tight contract for us, which cleared him of any liability for child maintenance etc., although whether that would stand up in court in the UK, I'm not sure. I know you don't do family work, but you're a solicitor... no, don't answer that! It won't be necessary. Anyway, he was there and every bit the person we thought he would be: tall, blond, fit, healthy, and very good-looking. A perfect donor really, or so we thought.

"When we arrived he was sitting in the hotel bar-cum-dining room chatting to Yannis the owner. He seemed really nice and it felt very strange, thinking I'd perhaps be carrying his baby in a few days' time. Only in the twenty-first century, I thought. Thanks to the net. It's quite something to put on social media, isn't it! Well, I haven't so far, and please don't say anything until I confirm you can.

"So we introduced ourselves, and he and Sean shook hands. We asked him to give us time to find our room, get unpacked and change, then arranged to meet him back in the bar again later that evening. I thought it would be nice to go out and eat together somewhere in the little resort, get to know each other; after all, that's what this was all about, knowing the father of my child, our child, Sean's and my child.

"The room was simple but nice. There are only a few here anyway, it's more of an apartment hotel really. Yannis apparently owns a villa up the hill as well. Anyway Sean and I showered and got changed. It's lovely and warm here in Greece, and the skies! Big, blue and sunny, with just the occasional fluffy white cloud. It's very beautiful. Whatever happened, we thought, this is a lovely place for a holiday. We could have, and perhaps should have, stayed in Corfu but we thought this would be a more intimate place to conceive a baby.

"Sean and I went for a walk to explore the little town. So pretty, with motor boats for hire, yachts at anchor in the bay and others tied up at the quayside; there are a few lovely shops here too and some really welcoming restaurants and tavernas. We stopped at this one, the one I'm calling you from, it's by the water's edge and just perfect. I could spend hours here just watching the world go by.

"We soon saw Svend walking along the quay and invited him to join us. He sat down and took off his white linen jacket, slightly creased from his flight the day before. He reminded us he was thirty, and a doctor at Copenhagen's University Hospital; he was a junior consultant dermatologist. Turns out he does this a lot. He said he thought he'd got about thirty successful pregnancies going! He assured us he was very professional about it and also produced a number of letters stating he had no nasty diseases or conditions, etc. They were in four languages! He added that his parents were both very healthy, fit and disease-free as well. What could be better? Well, a lot as it turned out.

"As well as us, he said he was also meeting a Dutch couple here, and they were arriving the next day. Turns out they weren't sure where to meet him, and he suggested as he was coming to the island anyway, and they wanted the same week as us, they might want to join him here as well. He added that it was more conducive to conception to be relaxing in the sun and not having to worry about fitting in 'making babies' between shopping trips and work. It also meant that he could give us a partial refund of his air ticket, as the other couple would pay his return fare. Brilliant, a bonus of a couple of hundred quid. Well, that would certainly help with the pushchair, I thought.

"We decided to walk to a restaurant in the square where he'd eaten the night before and try the food. He said it was fantastic, and as we were paying it seemed a good idea. The evening was closing in and the town was lit up with soft, subdued light, creating a gentle romantic atmosphere. People were smiling; the evening was warm, with a gentle breeze wafting across the bay. A flotilla of yachts had just arrived and the quayside was buzzing with excited holiday makers and a keen young flotilla lead crew, sorting out which boat went where and tying the mooring ropes to the rings on the concrete quay.

"The restaurant had most of its tables outside. What a lovely way to live and eat, I thought. We sat in the square. Our table was close to the restaurant's front wall, and soon the waiter had put a clean paper cover over the table cloth and brought us bread and cutlery. We looked at the menu and ordered our food. Then I needed to raise the delicate question of when we would do the deed, when would Svend give us his sperm donation so that I could try to inseminate myself? As well as the little syringe thing to put the sperm inside me I'd brought an ovulation test with me, and knew that tomorrow was the start of my most fertile few days so we only had a short window in which to get this right. I decided to wait to ask the big question until after we'd eaten.

"The food arrived and looked really good; we were pretty hungry after travelling all day. Svend was telling jokes and smiling, Sean and I were pretty relaxed and pleased with our choice. If our baby had the donor's personality I would be very happy, I decided. He was clearly an intelligent guy as well. After we'd eaten our main course we ordered dessert. I had some lemon pie and Sean and Svend the *baklava*. Then the waiter brought us some complimentary ouzos with water.

"This was a good time to raise the question, I thought, but Svend beat me to it. He leaned forward and his voice took on a more serious tone. That's when the bombshell was dropped. He just smiled and said:

"'So, Claire and Sean, you are desperate for this baby, right? I can tell. As I said, I have thirty pregnancies to my credit and they have all started the same way, they are always successful, every one. I am as fertile as Freya, except she was female! She was the Viking goddess of fertility among other things. For sure, my sperm is as fertile and strong as you can get. The way I always ensure success is to make sure I put it there myself.'

"OK, I thought. Well, he is a doctor so I guess him pushing the turkey baster up there isn't a really big deal; he's experienced at it too. But that wasn't what he meant.

"'I always have intercourse with my recipients. I cannot afford to lose my one hundred per cent reputation and I want to ensure a baby is made with love. I don't mind if husbands watch or join in, or if the wife stays half-dressed or it's in the dark, but it has to be this way.' He stopped talking and took a drink, waiting for the penny to drop. There was a difficult silence until Sean said:

"No way! You're kidding, that's not going to happen."

"Svend then said, smiling as if he'd heard this before:

"'OK, if you want to back out I will refund your money. It's no problem. I have the Dutch couple also this week, so it's not a wasted trip.'

"'Why didn't you tell us this in the first place, Svend?' I asked, a little shocked.

"He replied matter-of-factly: 'Because then you would probably have said no and wasted a chance of making the baby you need and want. I know couples who are so desperate they will do anything. This is quite easy. I suggest we do it as many times as we can while we're here, as the first time you mums to be can be a little tense. After that you relax and are more likely to conceive.'

"'Wow!' I said, and added, 'Look, Svend, Sean and I clearly need to talk about this. I'm not sure it's something we can do. Can't you just give us some of your sperm and I'll try to impregnate myself with it?'

"'No,' he replied firmly. And added: 'It's the way I do it and, believe me, it always works. When are you most fertile? Tomorrow and the next few days? So we could do it tomorrow Monday, and again Tuesday, Wednesday, Thursday. We need to do it three or four times at least. The more you do it, the more of a chance you have, after all.'

"Then I said to him: 'But you have the Dutch couple here as well.' He surprised me and staggered Sean by replying: 'I could always do you both together, in the same session. After fifteen minutes I can be good to go again, with the right stimulation. I am not just a machine. The more excited I get, the more sperm will go into you, and also with more force and enthusiasm too. Believe me, it works. It's up to you. You can back out now and I will give you your money back, you can have a nice holiday and then think again when you get home to England. Let me know tomorrow. OK, now I will take a walk and leave you to it. A very good evening to you both.'

"We watched him leave, his blond hair and height marking him out as he threaded his way through the tables and down the narrow street into the night. Neither of us spoke, just stared into our empty glasses. The waiter brought the bill. Then a voice cut through my gloom.

"'Claire! Claire, it IS you!' Remember I told you about Emily? We did our accountancy exams together and worked for the same firm for five years? Yes, her. Well, I told you at the time, she went to Australia with her boyfriend… he was a dentist… yes, that's right, you remember. I said at the time how jealous I was that she was starting a new life in the sun. Well, it wasn't all sunshine and flowers as they broke up after a year, but good old Emily pressed on and found a lovely new guy. She told me about him at the time and sent pictures. Sadly we lost touch a bit, the odd email but you know how it is.

"Anyway, turned out she and her Aussie hubby Nathan were having a three-week holiday on a yacht they'd chartered. They'd brought their three and four year olds with them, and Emily was pregnant again! It seems Nathan is as fertile as a dingo, or so she said. They were on the boat with her parents, so Emily and Nathan could spend some time alone together ashore. It was so good to see her! We paid our bill and went to the taverna on the quay where I'm sitting and phoning you from right now.

"She wanted to know what was causing the atmosphere between Sean and me; he was walking with Nathan, discussing cricket and boats, but wasn't being very talkative. So I told her what had happened. She said they'd planned to take the boat to the other end of the island the next day, Monday, but as we were still in the area, they'd come back on Wednesday to see us, and find out what we had decided to do.

"It was great seeing her and having another woman to talk to. She was so lucky! I saw them from the hotel balcony the next morning, walking along the quay, Emily and her mum and the two little ones. Beautiful kids... blond, happy, healthy. When Sean and I got back to our room that night we closed and locked the door, knowing Svend was just two rooms away. There was an older couple in the room between us. I went through such a range of emotions. In a flirty sort of way I'd actually persuaded myself to quite fancy Svend as well, and Sean was probably aware of that. He obviously felt threatened. How could I explain to him that I loved him, Sean, and wanted this to be our child, his and mine? I felt I was being emotionally blackmailed into sleeping with this other man... well, having sex with him... just so I could have a baby.

"It seemed so unfair. So many people had babies they didn't want, and I couldn't have the one I longed for. We had more than enough money, a nice house, good jobs... everything but a child. It could even break up our marriage. Then I thought: Look, three or four bonks, how long would that take? I could stipulate minimal contact... no kissing. I could stay dressed, well, mostly, and it could be in the dark. Just wham, bam, thank you, mam. Or rather, wham, bam, thank you, Svend. He'd get his thrill and I'd get his sperm, Sean and I would get our baby, and then our marriage would be happy again.

"I tried to talk to him about it but Sean switched off the light, got into bed and rolled over, saying 'good night' in a Do Not Disturb sort of way. I sighed, went to the little bathroom and took my third shower of the day. I patted my stomach, thinking that the next few days could see a baby start to grow in there. I ached to be able to say, 'Hey, world, I'm pregnant!' But would Sean let me? Was there a compromise that could be made? Maybe I could just do everything except allow Svend to penetrate me. Did he just get off on sleeping with other men's wives? Maybe he would let me take the sperm from him myself...

"I got between the thin white cotton sheets and watched through the French doors leading on to our balcony as the full moon travelled across the sky. The moon, of course, was female in pagan belief, a goddess, and I remembered the folklore about this and fertility.

"In the morning breakfast was fabulous: fresh bread, yogurt, fruit, honey... oh, Greek honey! Sadly the atmosphere between Sean and me was dreadful. Then mid-row we had to stop and smile sweetly as Svend came down and sat at a little table in the corner. At one point during our altercation, which continued in whispers, Sean was getting the next flight home, then I was going home, and then Sean was getting a divorce, then I was.

"An hour later we'd said all we had to say to each other on the subject so we each went for a walk on our own. He went up to find a lighthouse he'd been told about, I went to the port and sat here at this taverna. I watched the little ferry come in and tie up, and apart from the day trippers I noticed a couple of about our age carrying bags. They stopped near my table and looked at a map of the resort. I called across to them: 'Hello, are you looking for the hotel?' The woman said: 'Yes, we are, are you staying there?' Her accent was unmistakably Dutch. So this was Svend's other couple. I introduced myself then said my husband and I were here to see Svend the Danish doctor. She replied, 'Yes, we are too.'

"Should I tell her what Svend's modus operandi was? I wondered. No, I'd let him do that, it was only fair.

"A few hours later I went back to the hotel to find Sean sitting in the bar watching the TV with a glass of ice-cold lager beside him. Next to him were the Dutch couple. There was no sign of Svend. I joined them and said hello again, introducing Sean, but they'd already met him thanks to

Svend.

"The woman surprised me by saying: 'So you are going to go ahead and let Svend give you the baby the old-fashioned way?' I replied that I wasn't sure. Sean was listening. Her husband then said: 'I'm good with this; it's one or two nights of sex and then a baby for life.' His wife smiled and nodded and said: 'He's a handsome man, Svend, why would I say no?' and laughed. She announced that they were having their first session with Svend that night, at nine o'clock, in their room.

"I felt like I was in an online auction and the prize item was about to go to a higher bidder. However good Svend's sperm was, he could only make so much of it and, oh, this sounds awful, but it might mean first come, first served as it were. Should I leap in with a 'buy it now' offer and say I'd 'see' him first this afternoon, if he was free? Besides he wanted to know if we were going ahead, otherwise he'd give us our money back and default to just being with the Dutch couple as Plan B.

"Then Svend walked in. He was wearing an open shirt, showing off a bronzed body with muscles to be proud of, and a tight pair of jeans. Jesus, he could make anyone pregnant, I thought, and have to admit I felt a bit excited at the thought. Sean, though, got up and went to our room.

"I quickly said: 'Hi, Svend, don't go away, talk soon!' I went into our room to find Sean on the bed crying. I said to him we had to sort this out. I wasn't going to fall in love with Svend, I just wanted his bloody sperm then we'd never see him again. I promised Sean I'd change my email address so Svend couldn't contact me, but after all he had a string of other women paying his expenses to screw them so he would hardly need to chase me. Get real, I told my husband, this is a brilliant chance and time is slipping by. Every month I was probably getting less fertile, with fewer eggs and less probability of conceiving, so it was now or never.

"He reluctantly agreed, and finally said: 'Yes, OK, bloody well go and fuck him then, but please don't do it in front of the Dutch couple as well.' I went downstairs quickly and said to Svend: 'OK, you're seeing these people tonight. Can we do it tomorrow morning?' 'In the morning?' asked Svend, puzzled. 'Yes,' I remember replying. 'It'll be less romantic that way. I just want this to be as quick as possible, and please, no kissing.'

"He shrugged, smiled, and told me he did expect to be able to enjoy some foreplay. He wasn't a porn star; I would have to give him some encouragement. Oh, god. I thought I'd just have to tell Sean that Svend had been a dreadful lover, like a teenage kid, couldn't hang on, and that it was all over before it began.

"So what would I wear? I'd have to look nice and I'd have to excite him otherwise he might not give it his all. Plus it was going to have to be more than once. How many times would I have to do it with him? Oh, this was dreadful.

"That night we watched the Dutch couple eat with Svend in the restaurant that we'd sat in the night before, and then as we ate at a table a short distance away they went off together back to the hotel. The Dutch woman smiled and waved back at me as she grabbed Svend's hand and led him through the narrow streets. She looked great, wearing a short skirt, a tight open top and no bra. Well, I thought, she's out to ensure he'll give her all he's got. Hope he's ready again in the morning. Bugger, I should have gone first. I squeezed Sean's hand and smiled at him, telling him it would be OK and not to worry.

"The next morning we met up for breakfast, the five of us. The Dutch woman had already booked another session with Svend that night, same time, same place. I quickly reminded him that I could do the morning again, but maybe we should switch around the next day so I did an evening session. Svend shrugged and smiled, the Dutch woman looked at me and winked. She said: 'I feel pregnant already! Not sure yet but I bet I will be.' She put her hand on mine and said: 'Claire, he's very thorough,' and then smiled.

"Svend said he'd be ready outside our room at eleven. He drank his coffee, said goodbye and went for a swim. I smiled back, said OK and drank some orange juice. I didn't feel hungry.

"Sean said he was going out for the day; he couldn't bear the thought of what was going to happen. The Dutch couple told him they were going on an organised walk and that he could join them if he wanted. He agreed. We all left. I went upstairs with an hour to go.

"I remember my stomach was in turmoil and my head was spinning. I showered again; I got out my sexiest knickers and my skimpiest top. Under it I had on my new bra and just a hint of perfume. I sat looking at the door. Bed made, and body ready to receive his Viking sperm. I realised I'd gone from planning to do it mostly dressed and in the dark, to dressing like a seductress in broad daylight.

"He knocked, dead on time, and I opened the door. He came in and said I looked very nice. He then asked me to strip. Just like that. I was to take everything off while he watched. Tensing up, I let out a long breath and undid my top. He nodded his approval. I'm quite proud of my body as you know, Lisa, so when I took the bra off I felt OK. He smiled and said my breasts were very nice. I felt my nipples stiffen. I pulled my pants down and let them hit the floor, stepping out of them. He stood up and took his clothes off. He was bloody gorgeous, seriously. He was half erect, and it was very impressive. Then he said I was to lie down and play with myself! I winced and felt very embarrassed. This was something I felt uncomfortable doing with Sean, let alone a stranger in the middle of the morning in full sunlight.

"I lay down and started to touch myself, he came over but then I just froze. I couldn't carry on. I stopped, said I was sorry but I'd have to try again the next day. I thought of Sean and felt so bad. Svend shrugged and said: 'OK'. He added that I was being 'very silly and wasting a day', but if that was what I wanted it was fine by him; he wouldn't refund any of our money, though, as we'd started. I said that was OK, the money wasn't important.

"I texted Sean to say I'd backed out as soon as Svend had arrived, I didn't say how far we'd got. Sean replied that he was really pleased. He said he found the whole thing just awful. I waited until my husband got back and we cuddled. We went for a walk and he showed me the lighthouse he'd been to the day before. That night we ate at a different restaurant but saw the Dutch couple again with Svend, heading back at nine o'clock for her second try. Again, she and her husband were smiling. I held my husband's hand and mumbled: 'I have to do it tomorrow, Sean, I have to. I really, really want that baby.'

"Wednesday morning's breakfast was almost a repeat of Tuesday's. More smiles from the Dutch woman and her husband, and another greeting from Svend the stud. 'Eleven o'clock?' he asked. 'Y-y-es,' I faltered. But then replied, more firmly, 'Yes.' Sean winced. The Dutch woman had clearly understood our hesitation and asked: 'Would it help if I were there as well?' 'No, no, that's kind of you, but no thanks,' I replied urgently. She added that her husband had been with them when they did it and it had helped. She was well-meaning but no way was that going to happen in my case, any of it.

"At eleven o'clock I opened the door, knowing what to expect from the day before. I was wearing just a dressing gown. I was desperate; my body ached for a baby. I invited him in and dropped my dressing gown, standing there naked and waiting. Svend surprised me then. He grabbed my breasts and pushed his hand between my legs. I was taken aback as this wasn't what had happened before. I shrank away from him. I hadn't had another man for years and was feeling vulnerable and scared. He was also very big. He'd pulled down his jeans and was fully erect. He was huge compared to Sean, and I wanted to go gently, I did not want to be ravaged. I shouted: '"NO, STOP! PLEASE!' He did. He smiled and said: 'One more go and, hey, that's it. You are reducing your chances of getting pregnant.' He dressed and left. I thumped the bed in frustration. If I'd carried on it would all have been over in minutes and I'd have had a chance of having that baby.

"That evening we met Emily and Nathan as planned. Her parents had stayed on the boat again with their nippers and we sat down in a restaurant in a garden; it was delightful. As Sean and Nathan ordered food I went to the loo with Emily and told her the whole story. I gave her the details of what had happened on both days and how I'd backed out.

Emily said she'd guessed as much and that she and Nathan were really sympathetic. She told me motherhood had been the best thing that had ever happened to her, apart from finding her husband. Then, amazingly, she said she and Nathan had discussed it over the past few days, and would we like him to donate sperm for our baby? He was blond, healthy, had made her pregnant three times, but it wouldn't be an arrangement like Svend's. It would be as a donation in a yogurt pot, if we could find one!

"Fate's a funny thing, Lisa. An hour later we had washed out an old yogurt pot and Sean and I stood outside our room while Emily and Nathan were inside, putting some of his sperm into the pot. They left, laughing happily, and said: 'It's on the table by the bed. Hurry up and get it while it's hot!'

"I told Sean to strip. I pulled my clothes off too. I said he had to make love to me first, he was the only one I wanted, and I wanted to make this baby with him, even if we added someone else's sperm afterwards. Besides I wanted my body to be as receptive as possible. We hit the mattress and made love. Afterwards we inserted Nathan's sperm together.

"Emily and Nathan came ashore again the next morning; in our room we repeated the operation. Then we did it once more that evening just before they upped anchor and sailed off to continue their happy holiday. So we hit my most fertile days.

"I think I'm pregnant! Obviously we can't be sure yet, but I am pretty convinced. Sean's happy, I'm happy, and we're back on track. I thanked Svend and apologised to him. He did refund all of our money before he went. Apparently I was the only woman who'd ever said 'no' or changed her mind. But, hey, it's worked out for the best as Sean's OK with this, and Emily and Nathan said we can always go and see them in Australia for a re-run if it hasn't worked this time.

"I can't tell you how glad I am we bumped into Emily or rather that she recognised me. Right place, right time, hey? I'll be back Sunday night and you must come round soon, we've got some celebrating to do! I'm in love with my husband again, Lisa, I have a happy marriage, and I'm pretty sure that I'm pregnant! I also know my baby's father, and that's really important to me. Hey, must go, Sean's arrived. Byeee!"

The waiter at the taverna by the sea watched as the woman put her phone back into her handbag, stood up, patted her stomach and gave her husband a huge hug. Together they walked off, leaving the table empty, ready for the next customer.

Back to the Start

The waiter at the taverna near the water watched a woman sit down at the table on the front. She was in her mid or maybe late forties, with mousy hair and a slight suntan from being in Greece for a few days. She was playing with her wedding ring, her expression anxious, and her eyes constantly scanned the bay where yachts were coming in or setting sail, heading out to sea and further adventures. He could almost hear her restless thoughts.

I love this view, it's beautiful: the strong sunlight picking out the lines of the hills across the bay; the exposed rock face sweeping down to meet the water below. White hulls and white sails against the gently dancing blue... Ah, another boat's arriving. Is this him? No, it's not his yacht, not this time.

I sit here watching, wondering if he'll actually show up, and if we'll really do it, after all this time, all these dreams. If we'll go back to being lovers, and I'll throw everything else away to be with him. Everything: my life so far, my husband, our friends, my job, the house... maybe it'll all go. I have to prepare myself for that. But it might be worth it, finally to put something right and answer the question that haunts me. Would I be happier if I returned to my first love?

I've just walked out on my husband, to chase a dream which quite possibly I should have surrendered twenty-five years ago. Maybe it was never meant to be, maybe I've just made a big fool of myself, but then perhaps I walked out because I needed to. We've finally got the chance to take it back to the start, before we took a wrong turn and headed off to live separate lives.

Here comes the waiter with my second drink; a cappuccino this time. I daren't have another glass of wine, it's only midday and I need to be alert. What happens if he doesn't show? Do I meekly go back to my husband, waiting for the airport coach outside the apartment, and beg him to take me back? Can I? Should I? I'll know very soon, I guess. God, this is hard.

It's hot today, 38 degrees! But then it's summer, the Ionian sun beating down as it always has. Above me another plane slides effortlessly through the cloudless sky, lining up for a landing; bringing in the next load of sun-seekers, longing for an escape, desperate for sun and tranquility, just like my husband and I were two weeks ago. I had no idea then of the meeting that lay ahead of me, as if it was fated to happen.

This all started way back at university. It was smaller then, my old uni, with just a few thousand students. I remember seeing him across the lecture theatre during those first few weeks of term. He was a second year and I was a fresher, but we were doing the same module, Anthropology. It sounded fun, all those tales of naked bushmen and strange customs.

I remember following him to the Students' Union café and sitting nearby.

Watching him with his friends, the union "trendies"; they were all outgoing, confident types, the ones who ran the entertainments committee, the debating society and the rest. He was the guy who introduced the groups on stage on gig nights, and sometimes stood in for the DJ at the hall of residence discos.

Three weeks later I found myself at the same party as him in the hall bar. It was hot and heaving in there; there was a smell of booze and smoke and hormone-charged bodies, the ever-present, effervescent hint of sex to come. The disco pounded out the usual songs. I danced with the throng and unexpectedly found myself next to him, smiling and nodding.

When he noticed me I opened my mouth and touched my lips with my tongue, trying to look enticing and interesting. It worked. He moved towards me and we danced together. The changing lights bathed our faces with the full spectrum of colours, each change a different scenario waiting to be played out; each pounding new song a story in itself, with multiple beginnings and endless endings. Then that track: "Let's Spend the Night Together". We danced, we flirted, told each other the highlights of our lives so far, and flirted some more. Then he asked me if I wanted to go back to his room. He said we could "chase the night", see where it led. I nodded, smiling, giving myself over to whatever fate might bring. This was like a dream. I was with him, and he was with me. At last. A long, lust-hungry night was about to play out in his passion-worn bed, us together.

It was a night of love, a night of fun, a night of sublime lust… two new lovers giving everything in the pursuit of pleasure, each of us ensuring it was as good as it could be for our new partner. The daytime distractions crept in on us with the weak winter sun. We were late for lectures but neither of us cared. The sheets were crumpled, the bed was a wreck, but we were happily entwined. He got up, but I grabbed his leg to pull him back to bed. I swam through the sheets like a mermaid stranded on white sand, and he came back to me, willingly. We spent the whole of that day in bed, unable to quench the desire that consumed and drained us. I was left exhausted, aching and sore.

He was the third guy I'd slept with since term began. It was what you did in those days... well, most of us anyway, apart from the ones who had boyfriends back at home. My student house was awash with different guys coming and going. Every week one of my housemates was in tears, about to be dumped by or to dump the guy who'd just been warming her sheets.

So we started an affair. Well, not just an affair, more *the* affair. We were the number one item, the talk of the Students' Union, the choicest item of gossip in the halls and bars. I wore him on my arm like a prize, parading him around whenever and wherever I could. Some girls looked on with envy; others with the knowledge that they'd been there before me, and knew I'd be in tears over him one day soon. But I didn't care. I wanted to enjoy it all while I could, live the dream, love the lust we shared.

As I sat, distracted, in lectures I could smell him on my clothes, almost feel him still inside me. Whenever we met he would walk up to me smiling, arms outstretched, and then the kissing would start. His mouth so moist and firm, his hands so soft and strong, and his fingers... well, his fingers, just knowing how, and when. It was so very, very good between us.

It didn't last, of course. We made it to the end of term and then, at the Christmas Ball, we said goodbye. I was too cool to protest. He said we'd run our course and should "leave while we're in love, no need for regrets, no time for goodbyes". We danced. We kissed. We parted. I cried. Oh, god, I cried. All that night and for many nights after it.

The next term he was already with someone else by the end of week one, but every now and then he'd give me a wistful glance, a longing stare. On the rebound I found someone else, a boy from my home town, a second-year student reading law; and that's how we got together, my husband and I. I stayed with him for the next two and a half years until I graduated. By then he'd been an articled clerk for a year with his first job in a local law firm back home.

The next ten years saw me do my post-grad teaching course, get my job at the junior school by the ring road, and my new husband and I buying our first house. Sure we were happy then with lots of friends, good money coming in; days of plenty; days now gone. Our first child soon followed and my husband got a junior partnership. Then we had the twins. There were holidays in France, Greece and Spain, new cars, a new house... it all unfolded exactly as it should. But always the memory was there of those glorious and passion perfect nights. Nights which would never return, but which had left such an impression on me that nothing else could compare.

Ah, here comes the waiter. *Yes, it was good, thank you, but I'm not hungry. Maybe it's the sun.* I smile. He clears the plates and smiles back. I order a sparkling water and still I wait, still I hope.

So the time flew by. I went to a university reunion seven years ago, and he was there. I'd gone because my best friend said we should try it, it could be fun. It was a chance to go back and see the places we'd hung around all those years before. That night there was a disco in the bar where he and I had first danced together. I danced with my friends this time. And then I saw him standing there. He'd come with his old friends as well. We both looked older, both a bit timeworn, but he still looked damn' good. I was embarrassed to think of the changes he'd see in me; my hair now short, my skin not so soft, my eyes less bright and my tummy hiding child-bearing scars under a baggy top. We didn't talk, but we danced. We held hands, our lips touched, but in a friends' not a lovers' kiss. I went back and danced with my girlfriends for the rest of the night.

The next day, on a tour of the new social science block, I met him again and we tried to talk. It was the embarrassed: "How have you been?" and "What ever happened to...?" and "Do you remember when?" conversation, played out between ex-lovers since time began. He was in TV, a successful producer of big network shows. Had won lots of awards, and met them all: the famous and the fun. I told him I was a teacher, married to my lawyer boyfriend. He nodded and smiled. Then we turned to go our separate ways but both stopped in our tracks.

I went cold. It was suddenly back: that light in his eyes, the softness in his touch. I felt my legs almost give way. I wanted him to take me there and then, anywhere we could – in an empty room, in a cupboard, in the loo. Just do it, now! He didn't though. We just hugged, and then he cried. I couldn't believe it. He said splitting up with me was 'the biggest mistake of my life', adding softly: 'I really loved you, you know.' He'd thrown me away, not realising what we'd had, until he'd been through almost a hundred girls and by then it was too late. Even now, two marriages ended and another on the wane, he missed me. He'd made love to actresses on passionate Paris nights; had famous singers throw themselves at him on bleached white sands; and he'd had secret affairs with models and footballers' wives. But he said it was me he missed, it was me he remembered, and it was me he should have married.

I was so happy, but also so very sad. I shrugged it off over the following years but it was always on my mind. I watched my husband get older, and fatter, and less inspired. It was all too comfortable, all too easy and we took it all for granted. We just stopped trying. Of course the kids did well and went to the right schools, met the right people, went to university and got the right jobs. I saw friends grow old, some move away and others change from the people I'd once known. My husband and I lived together but there was no spark, nothing to inspire, nothing to challenge, and no limits to test.

We came out here to the island two weeks ago for our second summer holiday. We usually have two in the summer, and then the annual Canaries trip in the autumn half term. Oh, and the skiing holiday every Christmas; every year, always the same. Except this year, when we arrived, I looked out of the apartment at the bay below and was drawn to the sight of a yacht coming in and mooring up. That was nothing out of the ordinary; the bay was full of boats. It was like a magnet drawing them in, a safe, protected anchorage. The quayside tavernas are welcoming and good, like this one, the one I'm in now, at a table by the water's edge.

I looked from the balcony in the apartment and I saw him. At once I knew it was him; it was his stance, his outline. I just knew. I watched as he dropped anchor. He was alone. I saw him look around, tie up some ropes, turn off the engine and go below. To be absolutely sure, I rang my best friend, my old university pal, back home. I asked her to do an internet search to see if she could find out the name of his boat. She texted me back. It was him. His name and that of the boat I'd seen had come up in a list of members of a sailing cruising club.

That evening my husband and I came to this very taverna, and sat at this very table by the sea, to have a drink before going to eat at the Italian restaurant in the old square. My ex-lover arrived by rubber dinghy from his yacht; he tied it to a metal ring in front of the taverna. He walked to a table near the bar and ordered a drink. I told my husband I was going to the loo and walked past the bar.

I stopped behind him and hesitated. I touched his shoulder and spoke. "Remember me?" I hardly dared say the words, but somehow they left my trembling lips. I smiled, and took off my sunglasses. He looked up and the expression in his eyes changed from one of query to surprise and then to pleasure. Tears welled up in our eyes. I gave him another smile, nodding and glancing towards my husband, still sitting at our table, looking out across the bay. I briefly touched my old lover's hand and walked away. I shut myself in the loo and cried.

When I came out he was waiting outside the door. This time we acted like lovers reunited. Clasped in each other's arms, we kissed. I allowed his tongue inside my mouth, the first person to do that since I'd met my husband. For a precious few moments we held on to each other and the memory of past times. We had to part, of course.

I walked outside into the gentle warmth of the evening air. I rejoined my husband and we finished our drinks. He'd been reading a paper picked up from a news stand, was cursing and swearing about cuts in legal aid, but it went over my head. I looked out over the water and saw my old lover heading back over the bay in his dinghy, leaving me once more.

I watched him tie the dinghy to the back of his boat, then climb up on board. How I wished I could have been with him. I thought of us hitting the bed together, his lips and mine joined, our bodies pressed together, hot and wet, holding, having, not letting go. But who was I kidding? He would no longer see the fresh-faced student that he'd bedded years ago. I had borne three children since then. In those days I was three bra sizes smaller and my stomach was flat. What if he hated what he saw? I'd feel so humiliated, so rejected, so lost. This guy had slept with stars and models, the beautiful and the best. Why should he look twice at me?

That evening I sat, half smiling and nodding, listening to the one-way traffic coming from my husband's mouth. We went back to the apartment, sat and read, and then he went to sleep. I crossed over to the balcony and looked out across the bay. There in the moonlight I could see my old lover's yacht, a small light glowing on top of the mast, it swayed gently in the night-time breeze. I could see a light on inside the cabin. Was he sitting up thinking of me, like I was thinking of him? As I watched from the balcony of the apartment, with my husband asleep in bed through the open doors behind me, my mind wandered. So did my fingers, pretending to be his, inside my dress, softly tracing their way down…

The next morning I woke early, my mind full of twists and turns. I went to the balcony and looked for his yacht. He was there on deck, just climbing down a ladder at the back into his rubber dinghy. He was coming ashore! I left a note for my husband saying I'd gone to the shops. I threw on a thin blue linen dress, bushed my hair and put on some make up as quickly as I could, not too much, just enough. I ran down the tiled stairs, my shoes clattering in the quiet morning air. I raced to the taverna by the water where I'd seen him the night before.

He was here, at the same table, his laptop open. He was drinking coffee and eating a croissant. I composed myself and walked over, my pulse pounding in my ears.

"Can I join you?" I asked. He looked at me and smiled widely, getting up to offer me a chair. I ordered a coffee and glanced round, worried that my husband had seen me leave. But he hadn't, we were safe for now. We talked about the island, the taverna and the little port. He made small talk about the weather and I asked about his boat. Then he told me he was living alone. His third wife had just left him for a younger man, an actor from a soap. His kids were grown up too. He'd even named his daughter after me. He was about to give it all up as he'd "had enough". The boat was his escape and he was going to run away while he was still young enough. I badly wanted to run away with him, but daren't even think about it for long.

Our hands touched. We sat there, in the warm silence, staring at each other like the long-lost lovers we were. A song came over the radio playing behind the taverna bar. It was one we'd known and danced to all those years ago, "Because the Night" by Patti Smith.

There were tears for both of us again as the lyrics found echoes in our hearts. She sang about the night belonging to lovers, as we'd heard her do so many times before. I reluctantly said that I had to go or my husband would wonder where I was. I wrote my phone number on his hand but begged him only to text, not call. He smiled. I left without looking back; I tasted my tears, salty and wet.

I got back to the apartment to find my husband still asleep, I felt cheated; I could have stayed at the taverna longer. Later he and I ate lunch at this very table and I felt cold and alone again as I watched my old lover's yacht move off and away. I saw him pulling up the sails and watched them slowly catch the wind. Then he was gone. Out of my life again, perhaps forever. It had been like a cruel dream.

My husband accused me of being grumpy and dull. For the rest of the day I wasn't great company, I blamed it on a headache from too much wine the night before. I said I'd had a few glasses after he'd gone to bed. Later, after he and I had come back from the taverna, I noticed a new text on my phone. I grabbed it to look. It was from a number I didn't know. It was from him!

Miss you xx, it read. I smiled, feeling like a student again. But it was a stupid dream; I had a husband, a whole life back home. The past was over. It was gone. But thoughts of him were still at the forefront of my mind and wouldn't go away, teasing and cruelly taunting me. I had to tell someone, so I took my phone and went for a walk. I told my husband I wanted to choose a restaurant for that night and go and reserve a table. I went to the square and phoned my best friend, the girl I'd been at university with, the girl who'd gone with me to the reunion, the girl who knew me better than anyone else.

I told her I felt such a fool, like a lovelorn teenager. Oh, why is youth wasted on the young? I asked her. Where now was the body I took for granted all those years ago? One that always responded as it should, always looked good, felt good. He couldn't possibly feel the same way as I did – burned out, used up. I told her about our kiss outside the loo. How I was in danger of losing myself to a crazy dream.

She told me I should come home and let things simmer down. I'd feel differently in rainy, cold England, with the gas bill on the mat and a dinner party to arrange. But I didn't want to listen, I didn't want to know. This was possibly my last chance; too much of my life had already been frittered away. I'd done my bit, raised three kids, been the loving faithful wife, turned up at the Law Society dinners and made small talk with the other partners' wives and husbands… and been bored half to death. Now I wanted something different. Was I crazy? Was this mad? "Yes, you probably are," she said. My best friend then told me to "get a grip", but added she would always be there to pick up the pieces, whatever I did.

So I texted him back, *Miss you too xx,* then added, *Do you think it could have worked? Us back then?* Soon my phone alerted me as his answering text came in: *If I hadn't been so stupid, yes.* I replied, *But you'd have left me like you left the rest.* He replied straight away. *Maybe then, but never now. I made the biggest mistake ever with you. Sorry, I never meant to break your heart.*

I put my phone back in my bag. My husband asked who it was. I said it was my best friend, checking how we were. We spent the rest of the day in a hire car exploring the island, driving down ancient lanes, past scrub, rock, and prickly pears growing wherever they could. We passed rebuilt houses and new holiday homes, some unfinished, and some looking like they never would be. We ate ice creams, walked around old villages and looked inside Byzantine churches, their thick white walls shielding us from the unforgiving afternoon sun. We went to a nearby cove and had a drink at the beachside bar. As we followed the coast road I looked out to sea, wondering which yacht was his; so many sails, moving slowly by, so many lives unfolding before the sunset ended another day.

That night I texted my best friend again. I told her how I felt: lost in a sea of confusion. I texted him too, somewhere off the island in his yacht. I said: *It's just too late now.* After a pause he replied: *Only if we let it be.* Then added: *But I couldn't break up your marriage, that would be selfish and cruel of me.* Without stopping to think I texted back: *What if we stole one last night, like the ones we had before?* He replied quickly. *Don't tease me. Stay with your husband, enjoy your life. Remember what we had. At least we had that xxx.*

That night in bed I was alone. My husband was talking to the couple in the next-door apartment. I'd retreated, telling them I had a headache. I curled up under the thin, tired sheet, which had covered a hundred holiday makers since the season began. I looked at my phone lying on the chair by the bed. I fell asleep.

A short while later I woke with a jolt. My husband was shouting at me, throwing my phone down beside me. I dragged myself into consciousness. It was one in the morning. He'd read all of my texts and knew what was going on. I was questioned like a guilty child, accused of this and that. Taken off guard, I cried and foundered, feeling guilty and treacherous.

I locked myself in the bathroom and sat on the floor, feeling cold and unloved. Then he said my ex was 'just taking advantage of an easy screw', adding, 'That's what men like him do. It's easy, you see. Except you usually do it with secretaries and office juniors, not married women on holiday with their husbands!'

I was surprised, and wondered how he knew about things like that. I'd done nothing wrong, but what about him? I came out of the bathroom then I became the inquisitor, demanding to know if he'd ever acted like that. I'd wrong footed him; his response was confused. I pushed harder. "So who did you take advantage of then?"

Turned out he'd had a one-night stand with an articled clerk before she left the firm. Then his office manager and he had, in his words: 'Messed about a bit, but nothing serious, just a bit of fun really.'

I faced up to him, only inches away. It was my turn to be furious now. He'd accused me of wanting to see an old boyfriend, a former lover, when he was actually admitting to having lovers after we were married! *Messing about a bit* was still cheating. When he said he and his legal partners 'all did it', I saw red. I shouted, I thumped the bed and I swore.

The couple in the apartment next door closed their balcony doors which a bang, trying to shut us out of their holiday idyll. My husband's infidelity had started ten years ago when he became senior partner, apparently. He'd handled it well, covered his tracks so that I never knew. It was only happening at work, so why would I? God, how stupid I must have been.

'It meant nothing,' he assured me. Well, maybe not to him, but his having an affair, groping, screwing and having sex with colleagues, certainly meant something to me. We unpicked our marriage, found all the faults, argued, blamed each other for our failings and weaknesses, then shouted and argued some more. Finally, exhausted, confused and feeling unloved by him, I cried.

We struggled through the next few days, spending our time on different beaches. We ate together in the evening but rarely spoke. We slept head to toe in the bed; I kept as far away from him as I could. I called my best friend time and time again, and I texted my old lover on his boat. I told him that I'd learned that my husband had been cheating on me. I could be free, but only if he was sure I wouldn't be hurt again. Half an hour later my phone beeped with his reply: *Meet me at the taverna by the sea, the table at the front, on Saturday afternoon. But be warned: if you come aboard with me, I will never want to let you go.*

So here I am. That's why I'm here now, at this taverna table, the one overlooking the water. In the space of two weeks I've rediscovered my old love and learned that my husband has cheated on me with his office pals numerous times. If I walk out, where will I live? What shall we do? I will have to resign from my teaching job, but I'm supposed to give a term's notice. Will my lover even show? Will he be the dream I hope for, or will the love I believe I've found just melt away like an icecream in the sun?

The waiter has brought my bill. I put some euros on the table and look at my watch. My husband's flight will be leaving soon. I imagine him sitting in the aircraft seat, my empty space beside him, and just one of our matching bags in the hold. Then I see it, my former lover's yacht. And there he is, smiling and waving from the helm. The yacht creeps slowly to the quayside and noses into a waiting space. He throws a rope to a waiter, who holds the boat steady.

I walk towards him, towards the boat, like I'm dreaming, but I'm really awake. I carefully step on board. Above me a 757 roars into the sky, taking my husband back to our old life. Home. I pass over my bags. I stand next to him as he pulls in the ropes, thrown back by the waiter, and I watch as he turns the wheel with strong hands. The engine gets louder. We're heading out, bound for the open sea, no course in mind. Music drifts across from the taverna we're leaving behind, floating across the water, carried by the warm, gentle wind; these are new songs, current songs, but old familiar stories. One has a line about never being as young as we are tonight. I realise we never will be. It's now or never.

We both hug, we both smile, and I start to cry. Am I a fool? Today I really don't care. I just need to be in love; I need to be in love so much that it hurts. We can't go back, but we can start again. Sure, one day our sun might set, but for now we've the wind behind us, sunshine above us, smiles on our faces.

Most importantly, for the first time in decades I have love in my heart. Where will we go? How long will it last? It doesn't matter. Time together is precious; every day is a pleasure, every moment a treasured dream. Today we're just glad to be us. Glad that the night belongs to lovers. Glad to be together, and so glad to have the chance to go back to the start.

The waiter at the taverna picked up the euro notes and cleared the table by the water's edge. He glanced over the bay and watched a yacht head out to sea, the two lovers heading off for a new life based on an old dream. Together now, together at last, together, as it seemed they should always have been.

Westminster Wife

The waiter put away the clean cups and glasses, as he watched two women just into their forties, sitting at the taverna table, the one by the sea. One of them carefully checked the signal on her phone and then dialed. Yesterday he'd watched her sitting at the same table, alone and crying, but today she seemed calmer.

*

"Hello, Mum, it's me... I promised I'd call... Yes, you haven't heard from me because I'm in Greece, on a small island in the Ionian Sea... Yes, it's very sunny and hot, and I'm at a beautiful bar in a pretty little port. I'm staying at the local hotel. Yannis the owner is terrific, you'd like him.

"I wanted to warn you that you might want to keep away from the papers and the TV over the next few days, because I'm probably about to go ahead with something and there's going to be some pretty explosive coverage. They'll probably contact you for a quote. Dad would have hated it. In a way it's best that he's no longer with us to see it. Sorry, that sounds bad, but you'll understand soon. Oh, and warn my sister too. She needs to lie low as well. It might be best for you to go away and stay in the holiday cottage in Wales.

"It's a long story, but he's been unfaithful to me, big time, and... well, it's pretty unsavoury so be prepared for some shocking revelations. No, it's much worse than that topless picture of me in the papers. I'm sorry, Mum, but I've finally had enough.

"I'm phoning you from a new number. I bought a Greek SIM card, so the number I'm using now must be for you and close friends only, OK? He doesn't know it. I won't be answering my usual number until I'm home in a couple of weeks' time. My old friend Sue is here with me. She doesn't know the whole story yet so I'm going to let her in on just what's been going on. Then, unless she can persuade me otherwise, I'm going to spill the beans, all of them, however nasty they are. I'll call soon with an update. Anyway must go. Love you, Mum, just trust me. 'Bye.

The waiter refilled little bowls with sachets of sugar as he watched the woman end her call and place her phone carefully on the table in front of her. She monetarily brushed her hand through her lightly highlighted, soft, short, mousy blonde hair, well cut but recently neglected. She seemed more dressed for a weekend in London than a week in Greece, and, looking tense and nervous, she took off her prescription sunglasses, cleaned the lenses carefully and put them back on her head. Turning to her friend, a smaller woman with short, dark hair, wearing high quality but well worn and lived in holiday clothes. She smiled and spoke.

"Well, Sue, that's it. I've warned my mum and sister. You're my best friend, that's why I've asked you to be here with me. I'm going to need your help to get through this. Thanks for coming at such short notice. Let me start at the beginning. Have another drink and listen, this will make your hair curl. It was at the Party Conference last year that I first had my suspicions. It was just after Julie died… remember, my best pal who lived in the village? So bloody tragic, breast cancer, only forty-two. Awful. I was feeling really low as you can imagine. So I stayed away from the Conference this time. I always used to go along to them, especially in the old days. I was a party worker so I would man stalls and help out. I didn't really like it but I felt it was my duty as the MP's wife to attend events, like fund-raising dinners and the constituency charity dos and all those parties that I was expected to be at… you know, smiling sweetly and nodding at all the right times to all the right people. It's the story of my marriage really, doing things at the right time just to please my husband. I never used to be a supporter of his party. At university when we met I was a Liberal, but he was so charming and so nice that I fell in love with him and we got together.

"You know how it unfolded, you were there with me! I think you might have tried to warn me off him at the time. Him and his Rugby Club drinking pals. Sexist, crude, drunk, but I fell for him. Do you remember when we got married? Wasn't it awful?! I wanted a register office but, oh, no, his parents insisted it had to be in a church. My feelings didn't count. Then there were his relatives. Oh, god, they were dreadful. You know, I should have realised then what I was marrying into and called it off. I wish I'd had the guts to walk out, saying, 'No, I've made a mistake.' I should have married someone else. Do you remember the end scene in the film *The Graduate* where she runs off and catches the bus, leaving them all fuming outside the church? I just wish that had been me. But of course I did the right thing and went ahead with it.

"So as you know he became an accountant, but I wasn't allowed to develop my career. I wanted to go further in journalism. I'd got in as a graduate trainee on the local paper and set about covering WI meetings, school dinner ladies leaving, and the opening of bypasses. Then I was covering council meetings and court cases, and enjoying it too. If you remember, I told you about it at the university reunion thing we went to. Well, then I got a job as a reporter with the local radio station, and that was really good fun too. Remember I sent you a tape of my first live broadcast?

He of course became a partner in his firm like he'd always wanted to be. Then I got pregnant, and he said I should give up work to be a full-time housewife and mum. I didn't want that, I wanted to go back, even part-time, but no, he insisted. Why did I let him? I guess because all of our friends, or rather his friends, had 'stay at home' wives. He said it was important to help him build his political career.

"He'd joined the party by then, the wrong one so far as I was concerned, but he persuaded me it was the right thing to do, 'right' being the operative word. Anyway he said he would have a better chance of becoming an MP by joining them; besides his parents had been members all of their lives and knew a number of people in the party who would help him get selected one day as a prospective parliamentary candidate. So once again I swallowed my old principles and went along with it.

"It was difficult. His bloody parents were awful, and I always secretly disliked them. His father, the old-style army officer, and his mother! Mrs 'stay at home and make cakes', straight out of the bloody fifties. Christ, she made me so angry. I realise now I was sucked into living like them. They were establishment arse-lickers and I had joined them. That's why you and I largely lost touch then; he wanted me to have 'new' friends, his friends. There was always church on Sunday, joining the right associations, going to party fundraising dinners while wearing the right dresses. Mind you, life was fairly easy; we had money, a nice home... well, eventually, two of them. Once he was elected, of course, we had one in London and one in the constituency. Our daughters were sent off to that bloody horrible boarding school. His idea of course, I had no say in it. His parents paid for them to go to the same school as his sister had been to, a posh school for nice young ladies. I was a grammar school girl but the local state school wasn't good enough for his children, despite regularly turning out kids who went on to become doctors, lawyers and artists.

"Do you know how awful I felt, betraying my own children by dumping them in glorified kennels just because their father didn't want to have the hassle of bringing them up himself? I didn't have children for someone else to watch them growing up, but they were taken from me. I had to let them go, was expected just to knuckle down and get on with it. Why did I let myself get that way, Sue? No, don't answer; it was because I was weak and stupid. I'm changing now, believe me, just wait and see what I've been up to.

"Anyway, my girls went to some bloody living gothic horror school, where learning about old traditions seemed more important than learning about human rights; where learning to fight inequality and combat child abuse came second to singing hymns and learning all the words to the National Anthem. My girls would be trained up like *Stepford Wives*, happy to toe the line and knuckle down, and of course to 'love, honour and obey' their future husbands.

"Yes, you can tell, can't you? I'm returning to my old values and morals! Remember me in the first year at university, talking in that debate where I took a stance slightly to the left of Marx and Engels! Well, I've rediscovered the real me, and it's because of him and his bloody actions. You know, I loved him once, I really did, but he's betrayed me so badly I just want to destroy him now, like he's destroyed me. It's taken all this to make me realise what he's turned me into.

"Two weeks ago, when he was out, I painted the kitchen sunshine yellow. Just to show I was entitled to have some say in how we decorate our home. Well, one of them anyway. He likes plain magnolia… colourless and safe. Just like our sex life. I also annoyed him by reprogramming the stations on his car radio to Radio 1. All of them! I love new music, he hates it. It was just a little thing, a minor demonstration that I have a brain and my own tastes.

"You may remember he was selected first as the candidate for some northern seat his party hadn't a hope of winning, just to give him the experience. I remember standing there in cold streets, knocking on the doors of Labour supporters, asking if they might consider voting for the opposition. I became used to being told to go away in numerous colourful ways, if only I could have told them I agreed with them, but I couldn't/ Of course he lost, and lost badly, but the men in grey suits had noticed him, and he went to the Party Conferences, praised the right people and jumped aboard the right bandwagons, and eventually was selected for Fettingham. On his second attempt he was elected.

"So there I was, a Westminster wife, to be worn on his sleeve as a trophy at events and functions. He suddenly wanted me to do my hair more and wear 'slightly sexier clothes', to help boost his profile. Funny that. When we were on holiday he went berserk if I went topless on the beach or by the pool. Now he wanted me to be all tits and teeth, like a chorus girl in a stage show. I went to so many damn' dinners and ate so many bloody Black Forest gateaux it became a joke. Still, it was all for him and 'the party'. Not much of a party for me though.

"Things between us began to come to a head after the Party Conference last year. He came home and I knew, I just knew, he'd slept with someone else. I could tell. He was different; so bloody happy, and strutting around like a spring chicken, or rather a spring cockerel. I questioned him about it, asked him straight out, but he brushed it off, saying of course not, what was I thinking? So I let it go.

"He suddenly started staying late at the House of Commons. Committee meetings seemed to be cropping up in his diary more and more frequently. Then finally there was this 'fact-finding mission' to Turkey. The facts were that he was on a mission to have a fling with someone, and I was on a mission to find out who she was. While he was away I went to his Westminster office. Ryan, who ran it for him, was there, answering emails and adding diary dates. There on my husband's desk was a photograph of me at a party function, with him of course. Once Ryan had stopped typing I asked who'd gone on this overseas trip. Looking a bit surprised that I'd asked, my husband's assistant told me there was a party of two other MPs and their researchers. There must be someone else, I thought. I knew my husband's researcher and she wasn't going to be having an affair with him. She was recently married, young and very driven, but not like that. No, it was someone else, someone who'd been at the Party Conference, but who?

"I left the Palace of Westminster and walked along Millbank, past TV crews on St Stephen's Green lining up to interview some minister or another about the latest storm in a teacup. I shook my head, wondering how far my career in journalism could have gone if I hadn't so readily agreed to give it up to become a Westminster wife. Other MPs' wives had careers, some were MPs themselves, so why couldn't I have done more? Don't answer that, Sue, I know already. It was because I was stupid enough to let myself be moulded into someone I wasn't.

"I didn't want to go home just then so I caught the tube to Holborn and walked through the late-afternoon crowds. I found an old pub a few hundred yards from the underground station and went in. It was divided into small panelled rooms with beautiful etched glass; almost unchanged since Victorian times. I had a glass of white wine and sat thoughtfully staring at the free newspaper that had been offered me as I left the tube.

"'Minister Resigns' read the headline. I gave it a cursory glance in case it was someone I'd met. I knew him, but not that well. Mind you, there could be a reshuffle as a result. My loving husband had been promised a push up the greasy pole so it might just be his turn next.

"With his party in Government and the next election some years away, they could afford to try people out. Being appointed as even a junior minister would make his bloody day. So was I just being paranoid and seeing a rival where one didn't exist? Surely he was too cautious to put his political career at risk even if he didn't give a damn about our marriage.

"I left the pub. Rain had just started so I darted back to Holborn station. I headed to our Fettingham home rather than the London one as I had food in the fridge there, and I wanted a decent night's sleep away from the background sound track of city life. I left the tube and found a seat on the mainline train. Rain pelted the windows as we pulled out of the station heading north. Soon the suburbs thinned out and the houses became further apart. The graffiti alongside the railway track on sidings and bridges lessened as we drew further away from the city. Night closed in around us. As we hurtled into the darkness I called ahead and booked a taxi to pick me up from the station and take me home.

"I got out and ran up the garden path to the front door. The automatic light came on as it detected me; I put the key into the lock and turned it, pushing the door open as I did. The house felt warm. I'd only been away for three days but the mail was piling up on the mat. I picked it up and put it on the kitchen table along with my bag and coat. I switched on the kettle and turned up the Aga. Going through the post, I saw something that made me stop and think. It was an ordinary-looking official envelope but franked with a police constabulary stamp. It was addressed to my husband and sent from the South West, hundreds of miles away.

I opened it and found it was a speeding ticket. He'd driven past a fixed safety camera on the A303 near Yeovil. He hasn't been anywhere near

Yeovil, I thought, but it was his car registration number. The offence took place a day after the Party Conference ended, a day he'd told me he was still at post-Conference meetings. It had been held in York. We live in the Midlands at weekends and in London during the week most of the time, so why would he be near Yeovil when he was due back at our London house in Ealing that night?

"I took out a frozen pizza and put it into the Aga. I grabbed a bag of salad from the fridge and opened a bottle of Pinot Grigio. The wine was cold and very welcome. I ate and then sat in the bath, cradling my wine glass and wondering. The phone rang as I got dressed; it was him, calling from Turkey. God, it must be late there, I thought, they're two hours ahead of the UK and it's ten o'clock here already.

"'Hello, darling, are you OK? I tried the Ealing house so I guessed you were in Ftltingham. Ryan says you called into the office today.' My husband was clearly fishing. 'Yes,' I replied. 'Er…' Then I stopped myself. No, I wasn't going to alert him, I didn't want him to start covering his tracks. I wanted to give him some slack and see where it led. 'I was in town so I thought I'd just pop into your office and say hello. Just say hi to Ryan, you know, rally the troops.'

"He sounded relieved when he changed the subject and told me the trip was 'very busy but very interesting'. He asked if I'd heard about the resignation of the minister. I told him I had, and he said he thought a reshuffle was likely. There would be more changes to come, no doubt.

I said goodbye, put the phone down, refilled my glass and went to bed. The rain continued until just before dawn. My sleep was disturbed by the sound of raindrops hitting the glass of the Georgian windows. Who was she? I would find out, that was for sure.

"Morning arrived with a bang, or rather a boom. A low-flying fast military jet had passed overhead. The roar of its engine cut through the silence of the house. I looked at my watch and realised it was 9.15 I'd slept in big time. That was the upside of being a 'stay at home' wife, of course; it didn't actually matter when I got up, provided my husband's routine was not affected. Yes, quite! Well, that's all about to go tits up, isn't it? Like a lot of other things.

"Do you want another drink, Sue? I'll call the waiter… *Hello! Hi, thanks, can we have the same again, please? Thank you.* They're very good here, and it's so nice, I'll show you the beach around the bay later, you'll love it.

Anyway, where was I? Oh, yes. So then I went into his study and turned on the computer. I went to his diary shortcut, the official diary page as updated by his office and anyone else who plans our lives, and I checked on his recent meetings. Nothing unusual there; he'd called in to see our girls when he was passing their school a few times, seemed to have gone out of his way to visit them, but they are our daughters after all, and the school loves having MPs' children there. It's a good conversational gambit for the Head Mistress. He'd also had quite a few meetings with that new women's Issues committee member, but she was gay, I thought. Couldn't be her then. There were two or three meetings with that TV reporter. She wears really tight clothes, looks good in them too, but she's always around the Westminster village, ear to the ground... perhaps bum to the ground too? I wondered. That was probably unfair but she was a possible candidate, as was the new researcher for his colleague on the south coast. Yes, I'd seen her at numerous dos, always looking keen, and with a body like a model's. I was sure my husband would be keen to get his mitts on her, given half a chance. I considered them all, and more. Then it struck me: what about the constituency chairwoman? She was divorced, late thirties, attractive, her dad was a councillor, and she was always very friendly towards him. Let's see if she knows anything about speeding tickets and Yeovil, shall we? I thought.

"I went to the constituency office and there she was, behind the big oak desk, paintings of former party Prime Ministers on the walls plus a photograph from the local newspaper of her and my husband on the night he won the seat, beaming broadly, rosettes on show, glittering prizes.

Ah, here's the waiter with our drinks... *Thank you!* So, I tried to trap her, said I was surprised that my husband had got a speeding ticket, especially as he'd spoken up for lower speed limits in a debate in the House recently.

She was clearly unaware of the speeding ticket and looked surprised. I backed down when she asked where he'd been caught. I said I didn't know, he'd just had one of those letters from the police, and when I'd opened it I saw the words Safety Camera and put it back for him to deal with. She nodded and sighed. So it wasn't Mrs Rosettes then?

"My thoughts returned to the TV reporter. I went home after getting some shopping and emailed an old friend of mine from newspaper days. He was now working for one of the TV political teams at Millbank and would know of any rumours. I emailed and asked if he could meet me for a drink. He replied that it was great to hear from me again, and invited me to name a day and time. I suggested we meet the next day in London, near the Commons.

"My husband was due back from Turkey that night so I decided I would surprise him by being there at the airport to meet him, and also to see who else was with him.

"Sitting in the café near the Houses of Parliament I waited for Matt, my old colleague, to arrive. I texted my husband and told him I'd have supper ready, acting as normally as I could. Ten minutes later in walked Matt, smiling and a bit flustered as usual. He'd been chasing rumours about the reshuffle all day, but no one would speak off the record.

"'Matt!' I called out enthusiastically. It was good to see him again; we'd met briefly a few times in recent years, usually at political events where he was working. He kissed me on the cheek, rather warmly, I thought, and then he took off his coat and sat down. I got him a drink, and after the "How are yous?" and the usual catch-up small talk, I said:

"'Look, Matt, between you and me, and I'm trusting you on this, do you know if my husband is having an affair with anyone? Are there any rumours out there?'

"'Not that I'm aware of,' he replied, clearly surprised and wracking his brain to see if he could pluck anything from his memory.

"'Why do you ask?'

"'A wife's intuition, that's all,' I replied.

"He promised he'd keep his ear to the ground and have a chat with a friend of his who worked for one of the red tops, and who'd know for sure. He did say he'd heard that my husband would be given a junior minister's job in the reshuffle.

"We moved the conversation on and reflected on our time together chasing ambulances back in the day, and looking for stories in dry, dull council minutes. Matt was clearly pleased to see me and asked if we could meet for a drink one evening if I was free. I left the pub and went back to Ealing.

"My husband texted me to say his flight was on time and he'd be back later, so that evening I caught the Gatwick express from Victoria and waited at Arrivals for him. I was standing by the barrier with the drivers holding up name cards, next to anxious parents, lovers and partners waiting for loved ones to emerge. He eventually came through with the other arriving passengers, rushing on to pick up cars, taxis, buses and trains, all watched over by a stern-looking copper with a large gun from the balcony above.

"I surprised my husband with a friendly tap on the shoulder. He was taken aback, unsure why I'd come to meet him. I said I had missed him, and he seemed to buy that. He introduced me to his travelling companions and, no, it couldn't have been any of them, but I was sure there was someone. We went home, and I switched off as he droned on about Turkey and trade and security and god knows what. Should I bring up the parking ticket? I'd carefully sealed the envelope again with sticky tape so he might not even notice it had been opened. I'd see what he said about it when he read it later.

"That night I got a text from Matt. It read: *You may be right. My pal who's a political editor says your husband may have a "friend with benefits" as they say; apparently he was seen at the Party Conference with some woman quite a bit, a guest speaker who was banging on about morality and the internet at a fringe meeting. Not sure who it was but I can find out. He says if you want to talk about it give him a ring, he's always after a story!*

"So I wasn't going mad, but how to catch him and her out? The internet and morality, I thought. That night he touched me. I didn't want to be in the same bed let alone have any contact, so I feigned exhaustion and said maybe tomorrow. We went to sleep.

"The next morning my husband was off to the House where there was to be a series of briefings. An hour or so later he sent me a text telling me that he couldn't say anything but it was very good news, and I was to watch the twelve o'clock news. Matt texted me too. He said:

Your husband's a new junior minister with a brief to look into "the state of public morality". A bit old-fashioned but designed to appeal to the older, back-to-basics element of the party, I guess. It should be on the midday news.

Cheers, Matt.

P.S. Any more ideas on your mystery woman theory? Also I still fancy that drink, it was great to see you yesterday.

"You know what happened next, don't you, Sue?"

"That photograph of you all over the internet?"

"Yes, you're right. But what you don't know is that *he* put it out there, the photograph. He came home with a big bottle of champagne and some flowers; said we should go out to the restaurant round the corner, the Italian. He said we needed to celebrate his rise to junior minister status and promised me it was just the start, but he had to play the political game. He said he'd had a brilliant idea to push his profile higher than the other new ministers' and rising stars'. He needed the public on side for his cause, his new mission, to promote morality and clean up the internet. He could be Home Secretary one day, he said, if he got the right image and the right support behind him.

"I asked him what this 'brilliant idea' was. He said: 'Look, old girl, don't get upset but, er, there's a picture of you on the internet, on one of those put up your own pictures websites. I think the newspapers are going to find it, and I'm going to be 'furious' and call for an urgent seminar to debate the issues."

"'Picture of me?' I asked.

"'Yes,' he said, and added: 'look, don't be upset but it's one of you topless in the sea, one I took when we were first married. We'll both be "horrified" and the public will be on our side.'

"'ME?! *You* have put a picture of ME topless on the internet? To further your political career?!' I was furious, for real. He was right, though; the press printed the picture, complete with a discreet little black bar across my nipples. Above it the headlines read:

Minister's anger at topless wife pic!

"He was instantly up in arms and giving statements about invasion of privacy and how his wife didn't usually sunbathe topless, it was just a one off after she'd lost her bikini top. Bollocks! I always did it and I always do… well, when I'm abroad! Anyway he got his well-oiled machine rolling. The constituency chairwoman, Mrs Rosettes, spoke to the local press, saying how awful it was, and guess who else spoke out? The Head Mistress of our daughters' school and *she* had been the mystery speaker at the Party Conference.

"She was there on the news, banging on about how it was the job of people like her and teachers at her school to bring back decent moral standards, and announcing she'd been invited by my husband to help set up a conference on morality and the future of the internet. Her husband was a banker, and of course he was also a big donor to the party. And there was yet more evidence too. I searched online and discovered she had a holiday home near Yeovil, where she went when time allowed with her duties at the school. So she had been at the Party Conference and could have been in Yeovil with my husband when he got the speeding ticket. Then, the final proof... if more were needed.

"I rang my daughters at school to say not to worry about the press coverage. They were fine. They said their mum had attracted the interest of the other girls there as I was clearly 'very cool'. I asked them how their Head Mistress was, and they said she'd been away on a week's holiday, in Turkey, and had only just got back.

"I was just gutted. I'd thought he'd been having an affair but this proved it was real. I felt so betrayed. I realised I'd been used all of our married life to further his political career. You sometimes suspect but when the truth hits home it still hurts, it hurts like hell. I cried and cried.

"I went to have that drink with Matt and told him all about it. He was so sweet. His long-term girlfriend had recently left him because he was always at work, so he was in need of someone to unload on as well. That's when I came up with the plan for the trap. I told my husband I'd be going away to stay with my cousin in France until the fuss over the topless pic had died down. He said that was fine and he fully understood. He'd be busy chairing a meeting the next day with a few core people, to discuss setting up this big conference on the internet and morality and stuff like my picture. I nodded approvingly and asked who was coming, and he fell straight into it.

"'Oh, the Head Mistress of our girls' school, another MP... a cabinet minister.'

"I smiled and said I'd pack in the morning and leave at lunchtime. He said he might hold a meeting at our Ealing house later. I said that was fine.

"Well, I left, but I didn't quite go as quickly as he thought I had. He went to the House of Commons in the afternoon, and Matt, who'd been waiting for my text to say all was clear, called round to help me put my plan into action in Ealing. We left the house just in time. My husband and his colleagues arrived in a taxi just as we walked around the corner. Matt and I sat in a café a few streets away and we waited and watched on his laptop, because we'd left my laptop plugged in and on, in the corner of the sitting room, with its webcam sending images to a site Matt had set up.

"My husband's little group seemed quite happy. He was there along with the Head Mistress, his mistress of course, plus the other MP, the minister, whom I recognised, and the minister's assistant, a leggy blonde. Then another person came in. It was Mrs Rosettes, the constituency chairwoman. She was carrying a couple of bottles of wine.

"A takeaway meal soon arrived and they all ate. Matt and I moved to the Italian restaurant around the corner and ate too. It was just a starter, I was too wired to eat properly. After a while they turned the lights down and my husband and his mistress went out of the room together, hand in hand. They were going upstairs! The bastard. They were going to OUR bedroom as well; he was going to screw her in OUR bed!

"As they left the minister's assistant went out of the front door, leaving him with the chairwoman. They started to 'make out' as I think the kids call it today. Anyway, Matt and I left the restaurant and walked round to the back of the house. He stayed outside with my laptop while I gently unlocked the door and went in. Matt had set me up with a small go-pro camera and recorder, which he'd borrowed from work.

"I crept through the kitchen and went up the stairs, gingerly, with my heart racing, my pulse thumping through my head. Hardly daring to breathe in case I made a noise, I pointed the camera in front of me and walked along the landing. Then, holding my breath completely, I pushed open our bedroom door. There they were, on top of the bed, naked. She was all over him, and they were both oblivious to me. I held the camera up and recorded for about a minute, but it was enough, then I turned on the light, holding the camera towards them, and said:

"'Hello, is this what you mean by morality then?' They were shocked. At first, when he hadn't seen the camera, my husband said:

"'Look, stay calm… er… you have to accept lots of us do this sort of thing. I still love you, you're still my wife. Look, why don't you join us? There's room enough for three.'

"Then he saw the camera. She was trying to push her blobby 38Cs into a rather hideous white bra, the sort you'd expect her to wear. God, what did he see in her? His mistress screamed: 'She's got a fucking camera! Get it, you idiot, just grab it!'

"He shouted at me, climbing off the bed and grabbing for his trousers. 'Give me that bloody camera now. Come on, don't play games or you'll regret it. You're my wife, for god's sake, just deal with it. I'm a minister now and you won't ruin that.'

"I turned and ran, slamming the bedroom door behind me, my heart pounding as I scurried down the stairs as quickly as I could. I got out of the house, but not before I'd poked the camera into the front room, and quickly asked the constituency chairwoman and the cabinet minister if they had any comment on the importance of honesty in marriage and whether they had a message for the minister's wife? I grabbed my laptop from where we'd left it by the door and then ran out as I heard my husband at the top of the stairs. Matt was waiting by the back door. We rushed round the corner and jogged towards the tube as if all the hounds of hell were chasing us. We ran into North Ealing station and jumped on the first train. We got off at Gloucester Road. By then we knew we were safe, and walked to Matt's flat a few streets away.

"He downloaded the footage from the little camera, and put the files on to half a dozen memory sticks. He also uploaded them on to a password-protected site so I could access it and publish from it whenever I wanted. Then I kissed him. We both laughed and said we'd see each other soon. It was like Bonnie and Clyde all over again! But this time we were the good guys. I posted one of the sticks to your address, Sue, in case everything else went wrong. I needed to know someone reliable had one.

"So I went to Gatwick as soon as I could and sat in Departures until I could get on to a flight to Greece. I caught the first one yesterday morning and came here to the island. My phone had dozens of missed calls and texts. I was feeling a bit paranoid in case I could be tracked from it… you know, my SIM… so I posted the phone myself to our constituency home address in a padded envelope outside Gatwick. That's why I called you from that payphone, if you remember, begging you to drop everything and join me. Thanks so much for doing that. I needed some support. Glad you could get that flight from Manchester, and thanks for bringing me some clothes! I bought a Greek pay- as-you-go mobile at the airport when I landed.

"Matt and his Fleet Street editor friend are ready to ask my husband, the Head Mistress and the cabinet minister some interestingly awkward questions, and to publish some rather revealing pictures as soon as I put them online. All they have to do is report that there are moving pictures all over the internet, allegedly showing the latest campaigners for public morals shagging each other and cheating on their wives and husbands and the press pack will do the rest. I'd love to be there to hear the questions!

"All I have to do, Sue, is press this button on my laptop here, and it all happens. I have to text Matt as well, to say it's started. He's going to have a very busy few days at work, probably covering a couple of Government resignations and another unscheduled reshuffle! There could even be an election!

Then he's going to fly out and join me here for a week or so. Well, why not? My marriage is over. I've already sent an email to a solicitor asking for an appointment when I get home to start divorce proceedings. Besides, Matt's much more my type these days!

"Oh, listen, how apt, they're playing Miley Cyrus's 'Wrecking Ball' on the sound system. Yes, he wrecked me, wrecked our marriage, so I'm going to be a wrecking ball too. What do you think, Sue? Do I press send and put the pictures of my cheating husband and his lover all over the web? Shots of his minister friend and the constituency chairwoman shagging on the shag pile? Go on, Sue, try to persuade me otherwise. Am I mad?"

The waiter watched the two women suddenly cheer and shout "yes" as they waved clenched fists in the air. One of them closed her laptop and sent a text. The other ordered champagne, and gave her friend a very big, very happy hug.

Cast Off Couple

The waiter at the taverna by the sea watched as a woman in her early forties, blonde, short hair, shoulder bag thrown over her arm, walked to the table by the water's edge and sat down. He recognised her as being one of the wives from the two couples who came to his taverna a few times every summer. She asked for a cappuccino, the same as she had ordered every day that week. Today she seemed happier, more determined and positive. He could tell she'd had a tough week. Six days ago he'd seen her brought ashore in a rubber dinghy.

The waiter had stood and watched as the man on board the small inflatable with her manoeuvred the rubber dinghy alongside the low concrete quay. He'd held the dinghy still while the woman climbed out. Without waving goodbye, she'd walked straight through the taverna and headed off to the small hotel on the hill, her bag slung over her shoulder and a rucksack in her hand. The waiter knew she'd be back. Soon the man in the dinghy returned with two other people and they tied up the inflatable and then walked off, a man and a woman in one direction, the single man going the opposite way. None of them had spoken a word. Not even to say goodbye.

He'd recognised them, of course. These two couples called in to the little port half a dozen times each summer, usually just for a night; that day a week ago, though, he could detect the tension between them. It was the blonde woman who was most troubled. He could tell she was agonising over something big, something that would change her life. Today, a week later, she was back in his taverna, alone, as if she had finally reached a conclusion. He could almost hear her thoughts as she mused to herself.

Two decisions, two directions… one might be postponing the inevitable, one might be irrevocable. Two weeks ago I thought the only decisions I'd have to make on this holiday was where to eat each night, what to wear and which island to go to. I've been awake most of the nights since it happened. The night she told us, I sat up until dawn crying in the cockpit of the yacht. I was a wreck, exhausted and confused; I still am in many ways. I feel like Caesar, I've been stabbed in the back by my husband and my best female friend.

It all seemed so simple when Joe and I bought the boat with Laura and

Ed. It's hardly simple now. At first I thought it was a joke, you know? We're such good friends, the four of us, so close and so together that what's happened is just gob smacking. I'm a bit numb really, and the person I want to talk to, the person I usually talk to about everything, is right in the middle of it. My husband Joe, my best friend, and he can't help me as he's up to his neck in it; partly responsible, in fact.

I've been married to him for twenty-four years. We've got two daughters, both in their teens. How will this affect their futures? One is taking A-levels next month and the other is mid-way through university. They think they're in a stable family with a loving mum and dad. Well, they are, I guess, it's just that their dad seems to be loving someone else these days. Why? Why now and why Laura? His job's going well. Yes, he's changed airlines, but as a short-haul pilot he doesn't spend much time away, unlike a lot of his other pilot friends on long-haul contracts. My job is good. OK, banking is boring but I'm often standing in when the manager's away, which is interesting, and they're a decent bunch, the people I work with.

Our house is nice… well, really nice. Then there are Ed and Laura. Ed is the manager at the local branch of an estate agent's, and Laura is an optician. They've got one son, Andrew. He's just started university, reading pharmacy, and they live two miles away from us, on that new estate up by the ring road.

The four of us have been friendly for years. When did we start being friends? Oh, yes, it was at that party to celebrate the Millennium, the one thrown by the car club. We had old Triumphs, didn't we? They had a Herald and we had a 2,000. I'm glad they've both gone really, those cars, they were good fun at the time but pretty dated and always needing TLC.

We got on so well, the four of us. We went on those holidays to Spain and then we had that sailing holiday here in Greece, and on one particularly drunken night we decided it was so good here we'd buy our own boat and keep her here. We'd already seen her, tied to the quayside in Sivota on the island of Lefkas, with a "For Sale" sign displayed on her bow. When we jokingly asked the owners, who were sitting on deck how much they were selling her for, we were taken aback, and the next morning we bought her, or agreed to buy her.

Since then over the last four years we've had every holiday here together on the boat, two each summer, one at the start and one at the end, when it's a bit cooler and quieter. It's been brilliant, and each summer we've seen new islands, new places and had new experiences. Sharing the costs and the work, a great little project. Then Joe and Laura, Ed's wife, went and ruined it by sharing another new experience. Shagging. I wish I knew who took the lead. They both say it "just happened" but, hey, someone has to touch someone first. The question is, do I go, or do I go?

That is, after all, why I booked myself into the little hotel, to decide what I'd do before we went home. I've either got to tell the girls and see a solicitor or come to some other decision... what, I'm not sure. I do know that I have to make up my mind before we all meet here at this taverna in an hour's time. Then we have one more day here before we take the boat to the marina in Corfu and fly home.

Had it happened before, Joe and Laura having sex? We all messed about, went skinny dipping, sunbathed topless, even went naked on the boat, but there was nothing sexual about it. Nothing ever happened; we didn't see each other like that, any of us. Well, I didn't think we did anyway. That night a week ago when we came ashore here on our favourite island, Laura said that she and Joe had something to tell us. Ed and I thought it was a surprise meal or a new destination we'd be sailing to, but no. It was a bloody awful shock. I still don't quite believe it and half believe it's some sort of a joke.

We went to our favourite little restaurant, the one in the square with the green windows. We sat there and had the usual drinks, and then Laura said Ed and I weren't to get upset but she and Joe had a little confession to make. Ed and I smiled, half expecting them to come up with some big joke about having drunk all the gin or eaten all the chocolate. Some joke. "This isn't easy," she said, and the smiles began to slide from our faces. I suddenly realised the night had a chill about it and the wind had picked up. "Joe and I have begun an affair." She stopped speaking and sat back, waiting for a reaction, which didn't come. We all sat in silence, ignoring the waiter who came to take our order. The thought of food suddenly seemed less appetising. Then I broke that awkward eerie quiet. It seemed like our two marriages had suddenly gone into toxic shock and were about to be put on life support.

"Joe," I said, turning to my husband, "tell me she's joking. This is a joke, isn't it?"

He looked at me and pulled back as if he expected me to hit him. "Sorry, Michelle, it's true. I'm not sure it's an 'affair' as such, maybe an indiscretion, I don't know. But, yes, we have been... er... doing it."

"For how long have you been doing it with my wife?" Ed asked as he quietly fiddled with his fork, not looking up, eyes still fixed on the tablecloth with a map of the island printed on it.

"Since the first day of the holiday this year, although we started messing about a bit at the end of last summer," replied Laura for the pair of them. The lovers had put themselves in the dock and pleaded guilty.

"Why have you decided to tell us now?" I asked. Thinking that if they hadn't we'd have stayed blissfully unaware and life would have carried on without this sudden sharp pain to deal with.

"Because..." said Laura.

"Because..." interrupted her lover, my husband, looking at me "... because, Michelle, I love you and can't carry on doing this without you knowing, it's not fair."

I was angry enough to speak out by then. "It's not bloody fair, you screwing Laura, is it? And, Laura, it's hardly bloody fair of you to seduce my husband!"

Quickly she responded: "He didn't take much seducing; he was as ready for this as I was. Maybe if you'd had a bit more sex with him things would have been different."

"I struggled to choose between a) storming off after hitting one or both of them, or b) trying to find a way ahead before our happiness and our family life were completely destroyed.. An old song by the Gin Blossoms says something about it being a long way to fall when the knots we tie come undone. From where I was standing it looked like a bloody chasm, depths from which none of us might ever emerge.

"Hell, I was gutted. I was angry. I was distraught and shaken, like a building with foundations shattered after an earthquake. Nothing else seemed to matter but that moment. I started to imagine them together: Laura kissing him, Joe touching her breasts... No, no more, this is just awful, I told myself. How many others had been in this position, wracked by this torment?

"Have you done it often?" asked Ed, still looking down, tears spilling over his cheeks. I instinctively held his arm to offer comfort, the pair of us both victims and both injured; desperately hurt by our partners. Laura looked at him and grabbed his hand.

"Sorry, Ed. If you really want to know, then almost every day. Hadn't you both noticed how we'd suggest you went shopping while we would swim off together and disappear around headlands? And how we'd go off to have showers in tavernas at the same time? So we've done it on the shore, in showers, and on the boat, in both of our beds, whenever we've been alone. I can't give you an exact number of times. All I can say is that it's been really, really exciting."

I wasn't going to listen to any more of this. "I think I need some time alone with my husband, Laura, if that's OK with you?" I could hardly control my fury. Joe and I left the table and walked to the end of the village without speaking. "You absolute bastard," I finally said, having to hold myself back from hitting him. "Why did you do it? Just because she opened her legs? She's not exactly a model, is she? Laura's got the same stretch marks and the same post-childbirth body as me," I ranted. "Is this love or lust?"

He bumbled his way through an apologetic list of half-baked reasons. It came down to opportunity, motive and means, as the police say when investigating a crime, and he'd just confessed to a love crime of the oldest and first magnitude, that of being unfaithful. Laura was as bad. I'd thought she had a good relationship with Ed; he was always so sweet, so nice, so gentle and loving. Or maybe he wasn't. Why is it that nice isn't always enough? Why do "we" always want more? Why are we prepared to throw away everything for a few minutes of mindless, lust led sex?

We went back to the boat together, the four of us. Well, we had to, it was at anchor in the bay and we had only one battered dinghy between us. None of us spoke. When we got back on board I spent the night on deck, crying. Joe was in our bed, Laura was in hers, and Ed was on the middle sofa berth. I don't think any of us slept. The dark of the night and the pretence of sleep gave us time to reflect and absorb the enormity of Laura's announcement.

The next morning I was ice cold and calm. I packed a rucksack and told them I was going to stay ashore for a week, to work out when I was getting the divorce and what would happen next. Joe grabbed my arm and tried to hug me, saying it was unnecessary. That's when I slapped his face. Laura said I needed to calm down so I turned and slapped her too, really hard. She fell back and yelped. Ed asked if he could come ashore too, said he didn't want to stay on the boat like a gooseberry while my husband fucked his wife.

Laura and Joe both said they wouldn't do that, but I tugged Ed's arm and said, "Yes, come ashore with me, we can let this sink in together." Joe took me ashore first with my bags, there wasn't room in the dinghy for all of us and our luggage. We didn't speak. He then brought Ed ashore along with Laura. She and Joe went shopping; Ed joined me at the hotel. There was only one double room vacant so we had to share it, but with me in the bed and Ed on the couch.

The hotel owner Yannis was very understanding. He knew we were both upset, had seen similar things before. He could see my unwashed and unbrushed hair, my tear-stained cheeks and ruined make up left from the night before. I must have looked awful. I took a very long hot shower and slung on a clean top and some shorts. Ed did the same and I suggested we split up while we let things sink in.

I came to this taverna, to this very table, and Ed walked up to the lighthouse on the cliffs. As I sat at this table I watched Joe and Laura pull up the anchor and take the boat out of the bay. We'd agreed to meet again a week later, that's today, the day before we have to fly home. Meanwhile my husband and Ed's wife were off, no doubt for a week of wild sex, probably in our bed. She'd been hearing all of Joe's and my secrets, my likes and dislikes in bed, my weaknesses and fears. I was just so hurt. She'd been my friend as well. A good friend, I'd thought. How could she?

Ed was very thoughtful. He came and found me here at the taverna and bought me a salad for lunch. I picked at it; he wasn't hungry either. We went back to the hotel and sat on the balcony, watching the yachts come and go in the bay. What did he think? What did he want to do? Ed was as undecided as I was. We were both angry but he was more hurt if that were possible, deeply wounded. Over the next few days I considered all the implications of divorce. What would the girls think? Well, they were growing up, they had friends who'd experienced far worse, and it was a part of modern life. At least we'd lasted this long, until they'd reached their mid-teens; many other kids don't have that long with their natural parents. On the other hand, it could derail their exams, ruin their chances of getting to university. And there was that woman at work, her daughter still on anti-depressants five years after her divorce.

"Should we sell the house? We'd have to; neither of us could afford to buy the other one out. This was, I realised, a thought pattern probably being repeated by the other three, over and over again during the next few days. That might put Laura and Joe off their stroke! The bastards, why? Just why?

"That evening Ed and I came back to this taverna for a snack. They had pizza, moussaka, fish, salads, and a couple of other staples, so it was fine. Besides, the atmosphere here is lovely at night, full of life and happy people. Plus, on this occasion, two unhappy people whose partners had just dumped them. We'd been having the same thoughts, it turned out. Ed wasn't as concerned about his son as he was older and quite self-reliant, but the money and property implications were scary. Also we'd invested our lives in these marriages, planning to be with our respective husband and wife "until death do us part", to grow old together. We worked out that Laura and Joe must have been thinking about this for a while. How come Ed and I hadn't noticed?

We talked late into the night until the waiter said he had to close, and then we walked back in the chill of the evening to the little hotel on the hill. Ed gave me his sweatshirt as the wind had picked up and I was chilly. I had eaten and slept so little over the past few days that I was feeling the cold. I think Ed was too, but he was thinking of me. We sort of worked out that it was Laura who'd actually made the first move and that Joe was just too weak to say no. Or maybe he was so desperate to have an affair or to sleep with someone else he just grabbed at the opportunity. As we got to the hotel, Ed's phone told him a text had arrived. It was from Laura. She wanted to let us know they'd moored the boat in the small bay at the other end of the island and they both felt really sad about what had happened. Great, they felt sad! What the hell were we feeling?

"We went to our room quietly as the other guests were obviously asleep and those tiled floors are so noisy. The harsh white walls make any sound echo. We closed the door and turned on the dim yellow lights. Clearly this was a room where happy couples spent happy holidays. Happy until someone ruins it, ruins their lives. Someone they loved and trusted destroys everything they had.

"I turned on the electric kettle to make coffee. Ed and I sat in silence, watching the moon through the open balcony doors, the bougainvillaea blown against the railings by the night wind. Then he spoke.

"Michelle, can we just have a cuddle? I need a friend. I'm very lonely and a bit frightened."

I put down my cup of coffee and opened my arms to him. I hugged him like a mother would a child waking with a nightmare in the dark of a winter's night. Soon we went to bed, but instead of him sleeping on the small sofa I said he should share the double bed with me, just as friends, to sleep. My husband and his wife were sharing one of our beds on the boat for more than that after all, having a great time, banging each other and probably joking about Ed and me.

He walked across the moonlit room and climbed in next to me. We lay there holding hands, two victims of matrimonial deceit. Warmth and exhaustion overwhelmed us. We both drifted off to sleep for the first time in two days.

It was the little ferry sounding a horn to announce its arrival at the quay which woke me next day. It was eleven o'clock, I'd overslept but I clearly needed it. I got dressed and went down for breakfast, which I'd missed. But Yannis had kindly saved me some bread, honey, fruit and yogurt. I asked him how he knew I'd overslept and he said Ed had told him, and asked him to put something aside for me. I drank mugs of dark coffee and ate the lovely local produce.

Ed appeared then. He smiled shyly and came over to join me. He said we needed to go somewhere we could think clearly, try to take a break from this doom-laden atmosphere. We decided to hire a car and drove to the arch at the south-western end of the island. It was a beautiful natural feature, quite breathtaking. The roads on the island are delightful, narrow, winding, and bordered by rough scrub flourishing with wild flowers, prickly pears, cypress and olive trees. There are pink and white oleanders everywhere, the scent of the grass and flowers was lovely, and the sound of cicadas filled the air.

We stopped and ate at the island's capital, which was a little bigger than the resort where we were staying. We walked around the corner to the main square and had a lovely view of the quayside. Then we saw it. There at the end, tied with its stern facing the concrete quay, was our boat. Joe and Laura were clearly here in the town somewhere. We walked through the square and then we saw them in a shop doorway. We didn't want them to see us so we kept our distance, but interestingly we heard a row. The love birds were arguing. It made us both laugh for the first time in three days. The course of true love never did run smooth, I thought, and prodded Ed in the ribs, making him turn and smile at me. We scurried off, giggling, and found a small taverna on the edge of town. We didn't want to risk bumping into Laura and Joe again.

That evening we ate again at this taverna and then went back to our room. Ed asked if he could share the bed once more. This time he walked to it naked, and I was sleeping without clothes as well. It didn't matter; we were two friends in need of closeness and warmth. When we woke up I felt Ed's erection on my buttocks. He was asleep but I rolled over and kissed him on the lips gently. I thought, well, if my husband and his wife can play, so can we. He responded and I climbed on top of him, half wanting to get my own back and half wanting to share a moment of closeness with this lovely man. I gently held him and guided him into me. Without speaking, we enjoyed each other. I whispered that I was on the pill and he replied, "I know. Laura told me." We laughed together and then the physical sensations of sex overtook us. I'd given myself permission to relax and find solace in another man's touch.

Breakfast was lovely. We sat there, smiling and eating and feeling like a weight had been lifted from us. We had one more day with the hire car so toured the rest of the island, without seeing either our boat or our errant husband and wife this time. We wanted to tell the world we'd got our own back, but there was no one to tell. It was so quiet wherever we went. We followed a rough track until it ran out. After parking the car we walked, with just a bottle of water and a towel, to a tiny rocky bay with a shingle beach. We were alone there. We stripped off our clothes and splashed in the sea. Then, on the bumpy, lumpy beach we shared a towel and had sex once more. We had to stand up with me leaning over a rock as the shingle was too harsh and unforgiving for knees and bums! We were like two giggling school kids skipping lessons for an afternoon of sex.

As we drove back I got a long text from Joe. He said he'd worked out why he'd had this moment of madness; it was because both he and Laura had been "so sexually active from such an early age", and had had so many different partners when they were younger, that it had been a "natural" thing for them to just do it and have fun.

He added that he didn't want us to split up or divorce but maybe he could just sometimes be with Laura, to "scratch an itch", adding that he loved me and wanted to keep everything else as it was. It was stupid to ruin our lives just because of sex, he wrote, and it wasn't as if he'd slept with a prostitute or a stranger. Laura was "… after all a good friend and it didn't actually mean anything apart from pure sex". He then went on to talk about communes and other cultures where this sort of thing happened all the time. I showed this to Ed, who was reading a similar text from Laura.

We agreed we'd meet them both, as planned, at the taverna, this morning at eleven. Whatever happened, we had flights the day after tomorrow and had to get the yacht back to the marina in Corfu, which was nine hours' sail away. Neither Ed nor I spoke as we drove back to the hotel. We spent a few hours lying on the bed together, holding hands, talking about the past, our hopes and our dreams, and what we'd tell our husband and wife when they met us again.

So here we are, Ed's joining me in a few minutes and Joe and Laura will be here soon, I've seen them bring the yacht into the bay and drop the anchor. Phew, big decisions, big things to tell them. One thing's for sure, things can't go back to the way they were. They can never be the same again. For better or for worse, events have overtaken us and we are where we are. No, Joe. No, Laura. We can't go back, no matter what you say or do.

The waiter at the taverna watched as two people brought a small dinghy alongside the quay and tied it to one of the metal rings. He watched a man and a woman walk to the table by the water and join the other two people already sitting there. The two familiar couples were reunited. The waiter smiled, and when they were all seated at the table, he took them their drinks without being summoned, as he often did with customers that he recognised. As he put down their coffees he heard the conversation start. There was tension in the air. The blonde woman spoke first.

"Laura, Joe... Ed and I have been giving this a lot of thought. I know you both want us to go back to where we were two weeks ago, but that's not really possible. You've both hurt us a lot... No, let me finish, don't interrupt. I know you say it was just a bit of sex, only fun, but hey, that's not really the way it works. If all four of us had decided to do what you did it might have been different. It might be that way with some couples, in books and films and on TV, but Ed and I are not quite so liberated. Sorry. You two have made your beds and are going to have to lie on them. You've been lying on them with each other, after all!

"Here's the deal. We go home and go back to being 'normal', or as normal as we can be to the outside world. If you two want to go off and spend a weekend in a hotel, that's up to you. Ed and I probably will. Oh, don't look so surprised! And don't sit with your mouth open, Joe. YOU opened Pandora's Box! Or, in this case, Laura, you opened your legs to my husband long before I invited yours into my bed. Yes, we've slept together for the past two nights. It was you two who let the genie out of the bottle and now you will reap the reward.

"Ed and I have realised how close we actually are, and we're not just talking lust and sex here. It's much more than that. He's shown me something I've been missing… that's real affection and closeness, Joe, a closeness that's always been missing from our marriage. Ed will probably tell you the same thing, Laura. You two may have shared a spark but it's started a fire in us.

"I don't want to upset the girls so I want us to keep up the appearance of normality until Imogen finishes her A-level exams next month. I guess in time we'll play musical houses, with Ed and I living in one house and you two in the other. Once both the girls have gone to university we can reassess the living arrangements. This may not last forever, who knows? It's early days yet and we may even return to our original partners if we decide that's what we want, although at the moment that does seem highly unlikely. The alternative is two straightforward petitions for divorce, which will cost all four of us a fortune, and cause the sale of two family homes, disrupt three kids' education and cause even more heartache and pain than you two have already done. It's up to you.

"Now, Ed and I are coming back on the boat, but we will choose which cabin we want to sleep together in, so get used to it, and we won't be sneaking off to have sex underwater or in the dinghy or some damp steamy shower… we'll be doing it in the cabin. So put on headphones or sit in the cockpit because, guess what, Joe? Ed makes me make a lot more noise than you ever did! I hope you're happy, Laura, I hope your desire to have my husband shag you was worth it. Now come on, we've got to get to the marina in Corfu, and then go home as if nothing has happened and play nicely for at least two months. Ed, I think you and I are in charge of the boat from now as well as in charge of our lives. So Laura and Joe, how do you want to play it, do you agree to our rules or is it two divorces as soon as we get back?"

The waiter watched the four people who'd arrived at the start of their holiday as two familiar couples. They returned to the dinghy to ferry each other back to the yacht as two different couples. One pair smiled and seemed much, much happier than the other. The waiter looked forward to seeing them again when they brought the yacht into the bay for the start of another holiday later in the year, at the end of the summer. If of course they all came back together.

Backstage Backstab

The waiter at the taverna by the water's edge cleared away some old coffee cups as he watched a man he recognised as a pop star take a seat at the table by the water. The man had asked if it was OK for him to be filmed and interviewed there. The waiter had smiled and nodded. What he didn't know was that this was a much-anticipated interview with the lead singer and founder of one of the world's most iconic rock bands. It would reveal the real reasons why this epic band had fallen apart, and if they could ever play together again. In the hour that would follow, deep scars, backstage secrets, jealousy and powerful passions would be revealed to the waiting reporter and her camera crew.

"Great, yes, the camera's fine there. I checked with the taverna owner he's happy for you to do the interview here. He'll bring us some drinks in a moment. I've ordered a big jug of coffee and some biscuits, if that's OK? We've met before, and I've seen you on the telly! I Hope this table's OK for you. It's my favourite taverna, and this is my favourite island. I've got a villa in the hills behind us. It's a place I can escape to and enjoy the sun.

"So you wanted to interview me about the band and the big reunion? Hah, well, as you yourself know, I've always kept my distance from reporters, but now it's time the story was told. No one else will give you the truth about why we fell out, and why the big comeback tour may never happen. Our manager and promoter have been desperate for me to agree to it, as have the rest of the group, but hey, it's my band. I'm the lead singer and I wrote the songs.

"So I've agreed to tell you the story. Shall I clip this radio mic to my shirt? Yes, I've done it before, no problem. So this is an interview for the telly and you're going to hear whether or not I'm agreeing to a national and global tour. It's a world exclusive for you! OK… are you happy with the voice level, Ms Camera Operator? And you're running?

"Let me just talk then you can ask questions later. What I'm going to tell you may alter what you want to ask! So there we were, back together again almost twenty-five years after the breakup of one of the biggest-selling bands ever seen. Bands are born from a love of music, of freedom; from a creative powerhouse of passion. Sadly, they sometimes end up in court and in tears, and that's what happened to us. From hits and sell-out gigs, to distaste and distrust. We were backstage at that arena in London.

The gig had sold out just minutes after the tickets went on sale. Old fans, new fans, kids of the original fans, and the merely curious, all keen to see us back on stage after all these years. You were there? Yes, I'm not surprised. Hope you enjoyed it! Good.

"I remember thinking, that night before the gig started: In a few long minutes I will be walking out on stage again. The fans were waiting for us, for me, for our hits. Once again the Dream Daggers were going to rock the world. Our original drummer died seventeen years ago, you know, unexpectedly in the night. I got a call at four a.m. from a journalist, asking what I knew about it. I hadn't even heard he'd died until then! It was hardly the rock and roll exit he'd have wished for. The papers speculated that it was drugs, a wild sex orgy gone wrong, a fight, suicide, alcohol. Nope, it was a stroke; just that. It might have been brought on by his lifestyle, but it was a stroke. Yes, he spent years behind that big hedge of his in that old rectory he bought in Essex, and yes, he was constantly stoned and his lungs were wrecked, but the death certificate said stroke. Mind you, trying to keep up with his young wife probably didn't help. She was his third and he had a girlfriend living there as well. All very rock and roll, if you like that sort of thing. Sounds too complicated to me. Sorry, back to the present.

"Now you're too young to remember us in our heyday, but ask your mum and dad! Back then we were the biz. Endless rounds of *Top of the Pops*, *The Old Grey Whistle Test*, festivals, stadiums and recording studios. The German gigs were the best, we were worshipped like gods there. Girls mobbed the stage, tried to get to us after the show... We could and sometimes did let them in. That's another story, though, and not for now.

"When we started out, jamming in my room in a student house all those years before, we had no idea we'd actually make it so big. Was it luck? Maybe, but my song writing produced a string of hits. First one then another, climbing the top ten and hitting the number one spot. You never forget your first number one, and then the money rolls in, big money in those days too. It was an endless round of TV music shows, interviews, photo shoots for *NME* and the daily papers, and the radio of course.

"Oh, yes, sections of the music press and some fans said we'd 'sold out', deserted our roots, we weren't rock and roll any more, we were pandering to the A & R men. Some of the music papers, which had loved us at first, started to knock us. We pretended we didn't care; it was water off a duck's back. We watched the zeros grow on the bank accounts, bought bigger houses; and then there were the French villas, the yachts and finally the island. Well, we actually bought two islands, if you count the lump of sand and rock a few metres from the main one. The thing was, we were in in the charts more than we were out of them.

"It was in the Caribbean, the island. I couldn't tell you how much it cost, it was just a done deal. We built a studio on it… a great tax loss, we were told. Sadly, that's where it all went wrong. We'd gone out there for the summer to write that *always difficult* third album. The first two had gone platinum, led to a world tour and six months in the States, where they loved us. We played a list of big stadiums, before tens of thousands of screaming fans; truckloads of kit being driven across miles and miles of open roads by a seemingly massive road crew, and at night an endless stream of soulless hotel rooms and motels. The stage set got more and more lavish too. We travelled in a bus or on a plane, not knowing which venue or even which town we were in, not even what day it was. I had to have a sign at my feet so I could shout 'Hello, Pittsburgh!' or wherever, so I didn't get it wrong. It all became a blur.

"I couldn't write or even get inspiration for new material. We needed to lock ourselves away and chill, regroup so I could start writing our next big hit album. It's not easy! The management and record company thinks you're like a gaming machine… they can pull your handle and a new song lights up on the screen and money comes spewing out of the slot below. But I was dry of ideas, I felt like a cash cow that had been over-milked.

"The problem with songwriting is that all of your big hit songs are about finding love and splitting up, about new love and new relationships, but by then I'd been with the same person for over a year and I'd run out of inspiration, run out of relationship to write about. I was struggling.

"Our girlfriends had come out to join us on the island and we all got on very well; too well. It was a fun few weeks, living the dream. We lazed around on our private beaches, being served drinks and food by our catering staff. We swam in our private Olympic-sized pool, and watched the palm trees blowing in the wind. We were pretty relaxed, all of us. The girls were mostly naked on the beach; we all were, soaking up the sun. No one cared, it was cool. Brilliant in fact. Yes, there were drugs, dope mainly. I never smoked that much because I knew my mind had to be kept clear. I needed to start writing again, to get those hits down on vinyl, to produce yet another top album, hopefully bigger and better than the last one.

"So I started breaking off from the routine of late brunches and sunbathing, and locked myself away in the basement studio. I would sit there on a stool, in front of me big mugs of coffee and pictures for inspiration: of former girlfriends, other musicians, capital cities, fast cars, rainy streets… anything that could spark a story really; anything that could begin the process from which a hit would be born. Of course they couldn't all be hits; some had to be B-sides, as we used to say when everything was on vinyl.

"I wrote pages of lyrics and tried to find riffs and chord sequences that would fit them. Sometimes it happened in reverse. I'd string together a chord sequence, add a few riffs and sing what came to mind… shopping lists, train stations on the Northern Line, anything to get me started. It was so hard! After a couple more weeks I had four or five songs I was ready to play to the rest of the band, so they could add their bits, throw in suggestions and see where it led. Find some solo spots and the like. Then we'd have got our producer in to work his magic.

"We had a good first session. The girlfriends went to the neighbouring island on a day trip and the band and I went into the studio. We spent twelve hours working on the material and it really seemed good, lots of promise, some real gems, maybe even the biggest hit yet. Suddenly it looked good again. After that I carried on working alone, writing more tracks and improving the ones we'd already worked on. It was tiring but worth it. Then came the fateful afternoon and evening when it all went Pete Tong.

"I'd been alone in the studio when I fell asleep. I'd overdone it and was probably dehydrated too; I had a headache that thumped and banged and just wouldn't go. I swallowed a couple of Aspirin to help shift it and poured myself a big glass of sparkling water in the villa's kitchen. I slumped down on a chair by one of the windows and watched the trees bending in the gathering wind as the sun began to set. Then I fell asleep.

"When I woke up I found someone had kindly put a blanket over me, and a pillow under my head. I stood up and stretched. I realised that my headache had subsided, and went to find the others. That's when I walked in on them in the big open lounge. The bass player and his girlfriend were naked on cushions on the floor, writhing around like teenagers on speed. That was fine, but they were also with my girlfriend. Mandy was naked and on top of him, and he was obviously inside her. His girlfriend was, well, let's just say she was joining in. I was stunned. Yes, we were rock and rollers, anything goes and all that, but this was just not right. It was one thing to pass groupies around in the back of the bus in the early days – it was difficult to fend them off! God, that's a terrible thing to say… groupies are someone's daughter, someone's sister, someone's friend. Yes, they were obsessed with the band but we used them even it was consensual. I feel awful when I think about those days now. This, though, was different.

"Mandy and I were planning a future. We'd been together a year and, believe me, that was a whole lifetime in rock back in those days. 'Hey, man, it's just rock and roll,' said the bass player when Mandy saw me and stopped smiling. She scrambled off him. I stood there, looking unimpressed. They expected me to be cool about it, to laugh it off or even join in then write a song about it. Other bands did.

"Hey, I was the lead singer in a huge band, with gold records, hit singles, sell-out gigs, millions in the bank… but I was jealous. You see, I'd never had a relationship like it. I really had been in love, and then it was ruined. Mandy was the one thing I couldn't share. She grabbed my arm and tried to kiss me, but I turned away. She threw herself at me, naked and exposed. I shrugged her off. She held my arm and said: 'Let's talk, babe.' I shook my head. The bass player shrugged his shoulders and said: 'Hey, man, it's you she loves. We were just sharing a moment, cool it.' His girlfriend started to cry.

"Yes, I know I was tired, strung out, but I felt betrayed by everything I loved and everything I'd been working for. Mandy looked at me with big dark eyes, her lovely long hair matted and unkempt. Her breasts were smeared with the other girl's lipstick, her nipples still erect. I shook my head in rejection of her as the tears welled up in her eyes. I shrugged her hand off my arm and pushed her away. She turned to the window and stood there crying, silhouetted against the moonlight.

"The bass player rolled over and called his girlfriend to come and sit with him, which she did. I looked at Mandy, naked and lovely. Was I being over the top? Maybe, but something in me had snapped. Maybe I'd finally grown up, maybe I'd got old, or maybe I wanted more than the rock and roll 'dream'.

"I remember it only too well, like it was last night. I walked out and got our housekeeper guy to take me in the boat over to the neighbouring island, which had an airport. He told me I was mad, it was dark by now and there were no flights. But we went. I reached the airport and sat up for the rest of the night, waiting to get on the first flight to London. I had to go via Miami but I didn't care.

"I remember walking into our house in London, seeing the post on the floor, the note from the cleaner saying she'd moved on, and I realised the house plants had all died from lack of water. I went upstairs. There was a chill in the air and the room smelled of her, of Mandy, of us, of a love now gone. The sheets had been slept in and some of her discarded clothes lay across a chair. There was no going back, though. I saw the poster on the wall and the framed gold discs. I'd broken up the band, thrown it all away, because I'd had a schoolboy hissy fit. But, man, she was my girlfriend. We'd planned to have kids one day. I couldn't get over it.

"A month later I'd done the round of solicitors and accountants. In the early days together we'd never have believed it could end like it did. They all blamed me and I guess they were right. *"Big Break-up!* was the headline in the music press. *The Dream Daggers Nightmare Split!* wrote the tabloids. Our manager told a press conference on the steps of the record label's offices that it was due to: 'Musical differences while trying to write the new album.' But someone, I don't know who, leaked the truth. There were pictures of Mandy and me together, at gigs, in restaurants and on red carpets. Then shots of him, the bass player, and his girlfriend; and all the lurid, nasty details. Reporters in back-street bars made bits up and quoted drunken roadies and cleaners who claimed to have an insight into our lives. They even called my parents for a quote. Someone talked, and I still don't know who it was.

"The island was sold. The album was never made. I've still got those five songs I wrote before the break-up. In fact, we were due to play one or two on the new tour. In the early days we didn't need to rehearse much at all; we were hot, full of confidence and determination. I always wanted to meet the audience head on, sing in their faces, feel their response, touch their love. Truth be told, though, I had diarrhoea all day and all night before that come-back gig the other week where you saw us play. I hadn't slept at all, and I'd been dreading it. I'm a lead singer but I've got asthma now! I had a tight chest and a sore throat after rehearsals. It was from smoking fags and a bit of dope, of course. I don't do either now when I'm on my own.

"The reunion was the guitarist's idea. He called me and said: 'Hey, man, let's reform… do a gig. It'll be great, just like old times.' At first I said no, but the others were up for it, and the manager was desperate. He wanted the money, of course. I wanted to prove to myself I still had it, and it was also for the fans, still buying our records and downloading our old tracks after all these years.

"So I agreed to do a small reunion before a tiny invited audience. We hired a little London club, no stage, no press. It was a cellar, a place on Oxford Street, lots of bands did try out gigs there. We played just six songs, the old hit singles. The audience loved it. Of course, performance is like a drug. Once I felt the sweat, experienced the adrenalin, saw the reaction and heard the applause, I agreed to do it again. Somehow I found we'd been booked to do ten nationwide dates, with a world tour in the offing. We were back on the radio. Our music was being played again and old clips were being shown on TV.

"The response and ticket sales were beyond anything we'd expected. They'd even put on extra nights in some arenas. At first we'd been booked into small venues and universities but quickly moved to stadiums. And the Germans?! Well, they were selling out major football grounds. I thought we might even be able to finish off that third album. I still had those five songs and plenty of new material in my head; besides the money was going to be brilliant.

"When you've tasted that rock and roll lifestyle, living very comfortably just doesn't cut it. I know you won't understand and it sounds horribly greedy when so many have so little, but I wanted to be super-rich again. I had a dream of setting up a Trust for emerging talent and helping to fund new bands through my own record label. Sure, we made millions over the years, but others made millions out of us too. There were so many hangers on. The management team, the PR people, the drivers, the cars, the roadies, the equipment storage and all the other stuff… you won't believe how quickly other people can spend your money for you. Plus there was the record company's take.

"On the old tours we'd paid everyone really well, but forgot that the wages bill kept ticking even though we were no longer playing; we had contracts that had to be paid up and people who had to be paid off once we dissolved the band. They're all my lyrics, you know. The guitarist added a few riffs but most of our songs are my copyright. They tell my story, my life.

"So then we were back together again after all that time. Almost twenty-five years after I'd stormed off the island and refused to look back.

"On the night of the come-back gig, the one you saw, the fans were gathering in the auditorium while we were in dressing rooms out the back. God, things had changed! When we were at the height of our fame it was bunch of hairy roadies who humped the amps on to the stage and untangled a spaghetti mass of cables, jack plugs and weighted mic stands. Now it's 'guitar tecs' … kids who've done special courses on how to set up the drums, measuring the distance between the hi-hats and the bass. The mics have changed too. Earpieces to hear the output as well! But, hey, I've changed as well. Now I want to drink water on stage, and no beer or fags. We used to smoke dope before we went on; sometimes the drummer and the bass player would take speed too. We were mild, though, by comparison with some… well, I expect you've heard the stories.

"When they first suggested the full come-back tour I laughed and said we'd better book village halls as we'd probably sell about fifty tickets, to a bunch of sad old gits who wanted to remember their long-lost student days. I was wrong. Those ticket sales were incredible.

"Then the doubts started. You see, when we were good we were really good, but now? I was old! What if I couldn't remember the words? Doing six of our greatest hits to a handful of people in a cellar bar on Oxford Street was one thing, but this? A ninety- minute gig? What if I got out there and froze? I could collapse; have a coronary, a stroke, or a panic attack. I hadn't played a proper gig for decades. All I'd done was make a guest appearance on stage, playing along on a track or two with other artists who liked to cover our old songs.

"You remember before the gig I'd been on TV, being interviewed about the old days, and of course about the split. I always refused to answer that particular line of questioning. You've asked me about it yourself before now. You did it a month ago for that news programme. So there we were with what was supposed to be the precursor to a national and then a major world tour. I, of course, still had one big demon to lay… our bass player. I can't even use his name. No, don't say it, please! Don't even mention him.

"When he walked into that rehearsal room before the first try out gig, I was amazed. His hair had gone, his belly was bulging and his tattoos were like faded squiggles on yellowing, wrinkled skin. He looked pathetic. I felt sorry for him. At least I still looked the part. Yes, I've aged, but my body's pretty good. The first words he said to me, the bass player, after all that time, were: 'Hey, man. I've got a great new riff for you to weave some words around.' We kind of got on. He was acting as if nothing had happened. I tried hard to do the same, for the sake of the band and the others.

"Then there was Mandy. I didn't know if she'd be at the come-back gig or not. She wrote to me once, telling me she'd married but that they'd separated. Her name was put on the guest list by the manager but I didn't know if she'd be there or if I even wanted to see her again. Could I forgive her?

"Yes, since then there had been other women for me. I'd even got married but it fell apart. No one could ever take her place. The manager put the set list together for that big night. It was a no-brainer really. We would start with a couple of the big ones, do the new material, more oldies and end with two encores, if they clapped enough. You know the routine, encores are a ritual. Keep the biggest hit to the end. You can guess the song we were to sign off with. Enough kids do a cover of it these days on those TV talent shows that seem to fill our Saturday night schedules.

I laughed when I first heard someone cover it. I'd agreed to it as there'd be royalties, but I thought they'd murder it. They actually did a decent job and it was good to know my lyrics were reaching a new generation. It got to number one as well.

"So we'd rehearsed for four weeks before the come-back gig, and then it was for real. In a few minutes I would be walking out into those lights again, a sea of faces turned to me, all expecting to hear the band as it used to be. I remember thinking: will they make allowances or forgive us if we fail? Or will they want their money back?

I joined the others in the wings; the fans were clapping, chanting our name: *Dream Daggers! Dream Daggers!* I saw the others gather in the shadowy lights of the back stage corridor as we had so many times before. The emergency exit signs threw a green tinge over the bass player's balding head. The stage manager shone his torch to guide our way. I thought, If she's there, Mandy, in the front row like she used to be, can I cope? Will I even be able to sing?

"When we were together Mandy used to turn up every night, at every gig. Smiling, tossing her hair, wearing a low-cut top; red fingernails, red lips, wet and soft. I wrote our last hit for her, and tonight I would be singing about a love that failed.

"I led the Dream Daggers on to the stage. The lights were blinding, the roar from the crowd deafening. We'd been through it before, though. Our new drummer had been in other bands and luckily was no stranger to this level of adulation. We'd auditioned him two weeks before the cellar gig. It was difficult to take over from a dead band member but he was doing OK and was very keen to please. Control and dominate the audience was the order of the day, make them beg for more, make them adore you. You're rock gods. Well, aging rock gods.

"There was a momentary split-second's silence as the crowd's roar faded in anticipation and the lights were slowly turned full on. I looked sideways and nodded gently to the others. The guitarist hit the first power chord and the amps boomed out. Cheers of recognition rose from the audience at the lyrics of the first song. I hit it as forcefully as I could, desperate to show I still had it, that I was back.

"Opening my eyes, I looked at the first two rows of the audience and there she was. Right at the front, smiling, nodding, knowing I'd seen her. She waved and pointed to her neck. She was wearing a necklace made from stones we'd picked up from our island beach all those years ago.

"We ploughed on, thrashing through the songs to rapturous applause. I did my bit in between, telling the audience we were glad to be back and thanking them for their support. Mandy and the rest of the audience danced and waved and pointed at us and cheered. Wow, they cheered! Man, it felt good.

"Sorry, I need another coffee. Waiter! Another drink for me and my guests here, thanks. It's OK, we can keep recording, I'm sure you can cut that bit out. Anyway there I was, giving them my lyrics, baring my soul. Mandy was looking at me and it all came rushing in on me. As the songs rang out I realised I was still in love with her. I always had been. It was only ever Mandy I'd wanted.

"After the last encore I almost fell off stage. I was shattered, totally drained. The gig was massive, a huge success. We walked back to the dressing rooms and there she was in the corridor, standing there. Older, bigger, but still Mandy. Then the bass player rushed past me and hugged her. That was it; I had to walk out before I hit him. I passed the dressing room, passed our manager who begged me to stay. I got the stage-door guy to get me a cab and left without saying a word.

"So last week I flew out here to Greece, my favourite place, to decide the future of the band and the tour. That last gig was a precursor, or meant to be; there are loads more venues booked, stage crews and equipment hired, the publicity has gone out. Tickets are in most cases completely sold out. I've had the manager warning me about the cost of breaking the contract, and the other band members begging me to go ahead. I had said no, and everyone was going to be stood down. But then I had an email, via the manager. It was from Mandy. She was flying out to find me.

Life's too short, and the band is too important, for you to turn your back now. That night on the island was the biggest mistake of my life and I'd do anything to turn back the clock. Blame the drugs and a misplaced sense of whatever. I'm truly sorry.

"She arrived here on the Flying Dolphin hydrofoil three days ago. I met her on the quayside but we didn't speak. We walked to the car and drove to my villa up there on the hill. I took her hand and told her:

'Sorry, Mandy. Sorry I reacted like I did. I should have been cooler. I didn't own you. I wanted you because you were a free spirit, a true child of the sixties, how could I ever have blamed you for that?'

"I started crying then, feeling such a sense of relief. Yes, a big hard man of rock, crying like a kid! And now here I am, admitting it on camera. I hugged Mandy. We stood there in the entrance to my villa and I kissed her. She kissed me back, just like she used to. We both felt young again. Having her in my arms again felt great. We tore each other's clothes off… oh, sorry, you'll have to edit this! Afterwards we talked, we cried, we loved and we smiled.

"Hey, she can tell you this herself. If you look to my left you'll see her, walking towards us along the quay. So here's the big headline then: Mandy and I are together again, and the band tour WILL go ahead. Except for the bass player, who's agreed to leave the band. He'll get his share of the money but a session man will take his place. I just can't work with him ever again. He'll get his share of the loot but not his share of Mandy. She's all mine.

"Now if you'll excuse me, I'd like to ask a question before you start asking yours. Here's a surprise encore for you. Mandy, hey, come over here! Join us in this shot, sit beside me… yes, here, at the table. You're on TV now, babe, they're recording everything we say. And before this reporter asks us anything, I want to ask you a question. Mandy, will you marry me? ...I guess that nod is a yes! Hey, babe, don't cry, give me a hug. Look, I'm welling up too!

"There you go, TV people, an exclusive for you: the new Dream Daggers tour will go ahead, both in the UK and across the world, there will be a new album, and there'll be a wedding too. It'll be here on this beautiful island. Just how rock and roll is that?"

Behind the bar the waiter smiled and uncorked the champagne as he'd been asked to do. The reporter phoned her news editor; the camerawoman got as many shots as she could. The newly engaged couple hugged and kissed like teenagers in love. The waiter took his own picture on his phone for his friends. It wasn't every day you had the singer from the Dream Daggers and his fiancée for a backdrop, sitting in your bar, telling the world they were still in love and back together. The taverna by the water's edge was now part of rock and roll history.

Printed in Great Britain
by Amazon.co.uk, Ltd.,
Marston Gate.